Welcome to Maravilla

D0555617

Other Books by R. Douglas Clark

American Odyssey

Dangerous Crossing (Coming Soon!)

Welcome to Maravilla

R. Douglas Clark

To Liz & Jim with love,

Doug

BEELINE PRESS
NAPLES, FLORIDA
2019

Welcome to Maravilla

Copyright © 2018 by R. Douglas Clark

All rights reserved. No part of this book may be reproduced or transmitted in any form or by any means without written permission.

This book is a work of fiction. Any references to historical events, real people, or real places are used fictitiously. Other names, characters, places and events are products of the author's imagination, and any resemblance to actual events, places, persons, living or dead, is entirely coincidental.

ISBN 978-1-64540-064-6

To Shelley
For Shelley knows what
And Shelley knows why

Chapter One

All day at Julio's *barbería*, a gaggle of guys hang out, joke around, throw down insults. They talk about disputes between neighbors, criminal mischief, sports, political shenanigans . . . . They tell tall tales, lie about that time up at the lake, or embellish an argument that ended in a knife fight, or exaggerate how fast a hopped-up Chevy could go. Now and then someone would actually get a haircut.

If a short-haired woman should come by for a trim, the shop got quiet and the hangers-on shuffled away, got in their pick-ups and drove off. Those who really wanted a haircut would let the lady go first and pretend to read a magazine.

Julio's was in Maravilla, New Mexico, where women had tattoos and men had piercings before it was fashionable anywhere else.

One day at the *barbería,* the talk was all about a stranger who had recently moved to Maravilla. The rumors were flying, mostly false, but the truth was this:

Jacobo "Jake" Epstein, a lower-tier science fiction writer, earned most of his skinny bankroll by ghostwriting short stories for upper-tier science fiction writers who were too busy with more massive and "significant" projects to write their own short stories. Right out of college Jake had lived with his parents in Joplin, Missouri, but after some minor successes—a few of his own short stories published in obscure zines—he moved to New York City with dreams of becoming a sci-fi whiz kid.

Jake's first book had been popular among sci-fi fans. His second book had crossed over to the mainstream market, and it looked like he might be headed toward a successful literary career. But his third book, *The Ninth Paradox,* had flopped in the U.S., and was pulled from airport bookstores before he could say "tenth paradox." However, the novel was picked up by a Japanese publisher who wanted to use it as the basis for a graphic novel for teens. The publisher had insisted that Jake change the protagonist into a female, and Jake had agreed. The artist was an ace cartoonist, well-known in Japan, who turned Jake's mediocre sci-fi sludge into a visual thriller. Helped by some clever marketing, the book was a smash hit in Japan, and the publisher had asked for a sequel. Jake had signed a contract, with deadlines attached, and had received a smallish five-figure advance.

Perhaps because of the pressure of deadlines, Jake had trouble getting any traction on the book. He took to hauling his backpack into coffee shops to write. He became a coffee shop junkie, staking out his table early in the day, setting up his laptop, sitting, typing a little, sipping another cappuccino, keeping an eye on the bathroom traffic, Googling for bits of information, typing a little more, deleting the last line . . . utterly unable to block out all the distractions and thus utterly unproductive. Far from feeling like a promising young writer about to burst on the scene, he felt like a non-entity writing nothing for nobody.

After several weeks of coffee shops and nothing to show for it but a bad case of the caffeine jitters, Jake decided he needed a quiet place with no interruptions. In New York, this was about as likely as finding a yucca growing in Times Square . . . blooming . . . in the winter. So he changed his lifestyle. He began working at night in his third-floor apartment. He would work from dusk to dawn, starting after the traffic had thinned out and the construction workers had put away their jackhammers for the day. The city never entirely stopped, but the nighttime sounds were more peaceful and less intrusive. By the time the daytime clamor started up again, Jake was fast asleep with his earplugs in and a sleeping mask over his eyes. With this schedule, he slept until noon, and spent the afternoon doing errands or research.

But it didn't work. He still had writer's block.

Trying yet another tactic, he decided what he really needed was a work place away from his apartment. He rented a one-room office in Queens where he worked nine to five, commuting an hour each way like thousands of others. He bought a suit, a few neckties and a sharp-looking hat. He ditched his backpack for a briefcase. But this ruse proved to be no more successful than the coffee shop or the night owl ploys. His agent suggested a change of scene. Maybe he should get out of the City, his agent said, and move to the country for a while—thinking Woodstock or Provincetown. But Jake was thinking farther afield—not quite Greece or Tahiti—but totally different nonetheless.

Jake recalled the words of a poet (or maybe it was a travel brochure) describing New Mexico as "the land of enchantment." The light, said the poet/copy-writer, had a "transcendental quality" that invoked "divine illumination." That sounded just right to Jake. So he bought an aging Honda and headed west with only the possessions he could fit into his banged up beater: his laptop computer and printer, his guitar, an eclectic set of cups and glasses he had collected over the years, his favorite coffee pot, some thrift-store cookware, an ornate ivory-handled letter opener and a radio that broadcast nothing but static.

***

Jake found New Mexico to be exactly as advertised, especially in the north. The quality of light there was like nothing he had ever seen. Every leaf, every blade of grass stood out with microscopic clarity, and most days the sky was achingly blue. Of course, rural New Mexico and New York City were poles apart. They were diametrically opposed in nearly every way possible. They were black and white, fire and ice, dusk and dawn. Never and always. An extremist by nature, this contrast appealed to Jake, and he thought it might provide a spark for his imagination.

Jake rented a house in Santa Fe while he looked for something more rural. He liked Santa Fe but had his mind set on finding a place in the country, hidden away on a back road where he'd hear the birds and see more cows than cars. He found Maravilla by mistake, taking a wrong turn on the road to Taos. He loved it immediately. Driving down a narrow dirt road, essentially lost, he came across a property with a realtor's *For Sale* sign hanging on the gate. Jake climbed the fence and walked up a short hill to the house. It was empty and had the forlorn look of abandonment. Peering through the windows, Jake could imagine that with a good cleaning, some paint and repairs, it would be quite livable.

He contacted the realtor and found out that the house sat on five acres of land, some of it rocky and dry—a minefield of yucca and prickly pear cactus—and some of it suitable for farming. Sitting behind the house in a patch of tall weeds were two older cars, an Olds Delta 88 and a once-green Edsel, its chrome mouth fixed in a permanent "Oh!" of surprise. Each car had three flat tires, and one had mice living in the back seat.

He would have "water rights," she said, which meant nothing to Jake but seemed significant to the realtor. When he toured the house with her, he found it was an older adobe that had "good bones," as the realtor put it. Many things were missing or didn't work right, from doorknobs to light fixtures to faucets, but nothing major, except that it was in need of a better wood stove. It was up on a rise with a beautiful view of the valley, and Jake found it completely charming.

Jake bought the house and hired some local builders to fix it up. They spoke English to Jake and Spanish to each other. They arrived at seven and left and four, pausing at noon to eat homemade burritos, fat rolls of tortillas stuffed with beans and green chile.

Some of the electrical work required a permit from the county, but the electrician said he'd just work on the weekend, when the county building inspectors would be off. By Monday morning, he promised, there would be no trace of his work. "You can't get red-tagged for something they can't see," said the contractor. In return, Jake paid the man in cash.

Jake moved in a few weeks later. The previous owner had left behind enough furniture to get by, including a large wooden table that Jake set up in the front room overlooking the valley. Birds twittered all around, cars rarely passed by, occasionally a cow would bellow, or a donkey would bray. It was perfect.

With no more reasons to procrastinate, Jake set up his laptop and got to work.

Chapter I, in which Tai-Keiko, an adventuress on a mission, is rescued by a crone

Tai-Keiko stood in the shadows against a wall. She drew her Laser-Luger. Her spacebug had zero fuel, so there she was, stranded in a foreign city, on a foreign planet. The important thing, Tai-Keiko knew, was that she still had the Formula, coded onto a quantum-chip hidden just under the skin on her left wrist. Yes, it would be easy to detect . . . with the right equipment. A transducer could not sense it without a discriminator conduit, which was new and expensive technology.

Tai-Keiko had volunteered for this duty. No one else wanted to risk crossing the magnetic plasma field. No one else wanted to be powered out of the solar system into the outer galaxies where pirates from every crease in the space-time continuum waited to mess with you. And certainly no one else wanted to confront the Krossarians. They controlled the Orion region and were bleeding their planets to death, extracting all the minerals, even ferrazine, without which no planet can survive. Their greed and need for power knew no bounds.

*The Formula was brilliant: a toxic vapor that would neu-
tralize any Krossarian. The toxin was devised specifically to
contaminate Krossarians and was no danger to anyone else.
The source material was in the seventh ring of Saturn, which
was heavily guarded by the Galaxy Police. Tai-Keiko's assignment was to get the Formula to Zeton-9 and deliver it safely to
Commander Fallback.*

*The streetlight cast an orange glow. Tai-Keiko saw no one
in any direction. The streets were deserted. She scurried across
a road and took cover behind another building. Peeking in the
windows, she saw no one. She checked a few others. All empty,
all dark. Tai-Keiko knocked on a door and got no response. She
pounded on the door. Still no response.*

*"Hello! Anybody here?" she called out to the empty streets.
No one answered as her own words echoed back to her. The city
seemed de-populated. A ghost town.*

*The locator function on Tai-Keiko's resonance coil was not
working. "Must have gotten damaged in the plasma field," she
thought. So she wasn't even sure where in the universe she was.
An abandoned city? An abandoned planet? Tai-Keiko didn't
know what was around the next corner, much less on the other
side of this silent world. A squad of Krossarian guards had been
tailing her. She had given them the slip, but then her gravity
generator failed and she went into a hyperspace free-fall. Eventually she was pulled into the orbit of this seemingly deserted
planet. She had had barely enough fuel to make a safe landing.*

She was completely, utterly alone.

*As she had been trained to do, Tai-Keiko began to analyze
the danger factors that she faced. Need for food and water
topped the list, followed by lack of fuel. She didn't feel threat-*

ened, so fear was not an issue, although that could change if the inhabitants, or their enemies, returned. She half-expected hover-tanks to come swooping into the city at any moment. She strained her hearing for any sounds at all. Nothing . . . except . . . there . . . Was that a dog barking? At first the sound was faint and faraway, just intermittent yelps. But the sound grew gradually louder—yipping and yowling, howling and growling—until there was no mistaking it for anything else but a pack of dogs, wild dogs perhaps. Hopefully not winged beasts.

Tai-Keiko turned into a narrow side street, looking for an open door or window, looking for a place to hide. When she found that the street ended in a cul-de-sac, Tai-Keiko felt the first small shivers of fear pass through her body.

"Psst!" she heard. "Psst! Come in here, my dear."

Tai-Keiko saw a door cracked open. She could see nothing but darkness within. But the dogs were getting louder. What other choice did she have? Cautiously, with her Laser-Luger ready, she pushed against the open door. She entered slowly but saw no one. Behind her, the door swung shut and closed with a click. Tai-Keiko turned on the torch function of her gun and set it on low. She swung the dim beam across a vestibule.

"Over here, missy," said the voice. Tai-Keiko's torch touched a crone standing by a stairway. Her dark clothing contrasted with Tai-Keiko's white pilot's uniform, wrapped as she was in a black woolen cloak with ashen gray slippers and an olive green shawl over her head.

"Come, come! There's no time to waste," she said, motioning to the stairway. "Up we go."

The crone climbed the stairs, moving much more quickly than Tai-Keiko thought possible, and Tai-Keiko hurried after her. *The pack of dogs or wolves was much louder now, and Tai-Keiko could hear them clawing at the doors along the street below.*

After ascending two flights of stairs, they came out into a large room darkened by heavy curtains.

"You'll be safe here for the night," the crone said. "But we must plan your escape soon, unless, of course, you would like to declare citizenship." She laughed. "Though I wouldn't recommend it," she added, laughing again. "Germinal is not a very nice place to live."

"Germinal! So that's where I am. My systems are down."

"Yes, I suppose they are. I saw you land, my dear."

"You did?"

"Yes, indeed. That's a smart little spacebug you've got there. Not much for heavy lifting, though, is it? I imagine you took a beating coming through the plasma field."

"Yes, I did. I hadn't planned on running the plasma field, but I got blown off course by an unexpected solar wind. In this part of the galaxy the weather is so unpredictable. I don't suppose there's a repair shop in the vicinity?"

"Only for the overlords. We underlings must do for ourselves. We have our ways, though."

The crone began pulling out foods Tai-Keiko could not identify. She heated up an oven and soon the room was redolent with the aromas of good food. Tai-Keiko ate heartily and after dinner fell into a deep slumber.

To Be Continued...

Chapter Two

Maravilla was never a shining city on the hill or a happy hamlet in the valley. It was a phantom *barrio* of the foothills. Although it was as rural as a hayfield, any homie from L.A. with a certain haircut, baggy pants and a plaid shirt buttoned at the neck would have felt comfortable there, especially behind the wheel of a low-rider, *norteño* music blasting at full volume. Sure, the old folks had their own ways. They were the last generation to have spent more time outdoors than in. Their rough-skinned hands and weathered faces identified them as hardworking folks, bound to the land. Their anachronistic Spanish dialect marked them as people grounded in the past.

Why was Maravilla a "phantom" village? Well. Although it was home to 5,000 people in the highlands of northern New Mexico, the town had no legal standing because it had never incorporated. Years ago, when county lines were being drawn, no one stood up for Maravilla. Lacking the wisdom of Solomon (or even a chile farmer), politicians split Maravilla into two parts, running the county line right through the heart of the community. As a result, half of Maravilla was in Rio Grande County, half was in Carson County. Maravilla existed as a metaphysical construct, or an idea, but not as a legal entity. It befuddled mapmakers and confounded state officials. Maravilla, it might be said, was a living, breathing ghost town.

To add some mud to the muddle, both counties were mismanaged, corrupt and penniless. Whatever money the counties had was usually misspent, but it was rarely misspent in Maravilla. Conversely, if, say, a new playground was *not* needed in Maravilla, one of the counties would surely build one there. If a road had just been paved, the utilities crew would show up first thing Monday morning to dig a trench through it.

Anomalies abounded in Maravilla. For instance, half of the domiciles in Maravilla were trailer homes. They seemed to have been scattered around randomly, as if tossed there by a tornado. Some had an address, some did not. Some had a septic tank, some did not. These so-called "mobile homes" would never move again, at least not until several years later, when the insulation was falling down from the kitchen ceiling, and the toilet was constantly being plunged, and the all-weather siding was falling off like teeth from a seven-year-old. In that sorry condition, a trailer might be hauled away or, more conveniently, burned to the ground, as had happened recently, making a six-foot-high pile of black and burned-up rubbish with flat strips of metal sticking out, alongside melted wires and a charred television with an exploded screen. The cement block foundation was smothered in ashes and still-smoking debris. The owner of the cindered trailer cried "Arson!" because his insurance policy had a good arson clause, but the insurance company pointed to a stipulation that required the arsonist to be tried and convicted before that money could be paid. In Maravilla—split between two counties that were both broke—it was unlikely that the Sheriff of either county would want to spend the money it would take to track down the arsonist who burned down a crummy trailer.

Some of the trailers were made more permanent or more attractive by flower beds, carports and metal storage units. Sitting alongside the trailer homes were a comforting number of permanent houses, built from adobe brick and stucco. These houses were designed individually, each refreshingly different from the others, although they sometimes looked like armed camps due to the barred windows and coils of razor wire atop the courtyard walls. Given the jurisdictional disputes of law enforcement officials, locals had learned to fend for themselves.

The houses and trailers were scattered about on five- and ten-acre plots. Once upon a time, the land was used to grow crops, but as families procreated, the farmland was parceled out to siblings, and the crops were displaced by trailers. Property boundaries were marked by adobe walls, coyote fences or, most frequently, by barbed wire fences strung together between sticks two-inches thick. Most of the stays were crooked, but the barbed wire was well secured and tight enough to keep the fences from sagging. Some folks maintained that crooked stays were stronger than straight ones because they wouldn't split as easily. Mostly, the materials depended on what was available at the time the fence was built. Every eight feet there was a metal post pounded into the ground to support the wire and keep the whole wobbly affair from collapsing.

Anyway, the county line meandered its way through the village of Maravilla. Some houses had their kitchen in one county and their bedroom in the other. The Carson County side of Maravilla had good water but no trash pick-up. The Rio Grande County side had better fire protection but terrible roads.

The one thing shared by all of Maravilla was its post office.

The post office was in a tiny building run admirably by an omniscient postal clerk named Crystal. A dedicated civil servant, Crystal adhered to Post Office rules and regulations with patriotic resolve. If a letter required a recipient's signature, Crystal would not release the letter to the man's wife, mother or next-door neighbor, even if she had known them for 20 years. "Rules are rules," she liked to say, and who could argue with that? At the same time, Crystal always remembered the birthdays of her customers and sent graduation cards to all the seniors at San Ramón High.

In contrast to the order inside the post office, outside it was chaotic. The Maravilla post office had a small parking lot with no rules at all—no marked entrance or exit, no parking places lined off with yellow paint, no distinction between small cars and big trucks—yet there were never any accidents there. People were patient and polite, even though it was chronically busy all day long. The Maravilla post office was the one place in the village everyone went, and it was a sure bet that its patrons would encounter someone they knew. And whether that someone was a good friend or a sworn enemy, a distant relative or the devil himself, they would all be treated with respect.

The post office also provided a public bulletin board where people put up notices about lost dogs, hay for sale, *acequia* meetings, guitar lessons and so on. Right next to this jumble of information was the official U.S. Post Office bulletin board—a locked glass case that contained a tidy selection of postal news and wanted posters. Nobody paid too much attention to these dry announcements until the day a dispassionate item declared that, on the first of the month, the Maravilla post office would close forever. Throughout the community an uproar ensued.

This did not come as a complete surprise to the Maravillosos, for it had been widely reported that some post offices around the country would be closing for budgetary reasons. But no one thought they would close the Maravilla post office. The post office! It was the only place where no one was nasty and everyone was equal. It was an oasis of civility in an argumentative town. For this it was treasured, and nobody was willing to give it up without a fight.

The news spread through Maravilla like grasshoppers in a bean field. In a fractious community where disagreements were as common as burrs on a dog, it was remarkable how united everyone was.

Pilar Medina led the resistance. She owned a gift shop called Maravilla Blessings and did a steady business with the post office, shipping gift items all over the country. Closing the post office would severely impact the store. The next closest post office was ten miles away in San Ramón. But it was not only for selfish reasons that Pilar took action. She understood the importance of the post office for Maravilla: it was the village green, the town hall, the one place that belonged to everyone, regardless of the county line that divided the town. Unlike many villages in the area, Maravilla had no public plaza, that is, no square of shops and shade trees where people mingled. Like its residences, Maravilla's businesses were scattered about instead of bunched together. If Maravilla had a soul, Pilar knew, it was the post office. Close the post office and Maravilla would dissolve into a disassociated collection of individuals and families. Neighbors would cease to be neighborly. Hispanics would no longer talk to gringos. No one would trust anyone else.

Pilar organized a town meeting to decide what to do. Each half of the town had its own county community center, but Pilar did not want to appear to favor one county over the other. She wanted a neutral place, and she could think of only one such place that would be large enough to hold the meeting: Red's Blue Chile Tavern.

The bar at the Blue Chile Tavern was small, but Pilar knew there was a large hall in back that people rented for dances or wakes or weddings. She phoned Red Baca, Blue Chile's owner.

"Red, this is Pilar Medina. *Como esta usted?*" she said in her abrupt yet formal manner.

"*Bien*, Pilar. *Y tu?*" Red was more familiar, polite but a bit wary.

"Okay. You know about the post office closing?"

"I know, I know. It's a terrible thing."

"I want to stop it. We need our post office."

"*Si*, Pilar, *pero* what can we do?"

"To start with, I want to have a meeting for everyone to come and talk about it."

"Yes, that would be good. When is this meeting?"

"How about next Saturday in your dance hall?"

"Pilar, the dance hall costs $150 to rent."

Pilar could almost see Red's lopsided smile across the phone line.

"I don't want to rent it," she said. "I want you to donate it. After the meeting, you can open the bar and you'll have lots of customers."

"You want me to close the bar on Saturday afternoon and open up the hall for free?"

"That's right. It's your civic duty."

Red knew Pilar was right. He did not want to lose the post office either. So he agreed to Pilar's request. Pilar asked her daughter Paloma to make a sign for the community bulletin board at the post office to announce the meeting. Paloma also made flyers to tack up on telephone poles and tape to store windows. It wasn't long before everyone in town knew about the meeting.

Chapter Three

Jake had purchased his land in Maravilla from a woman who lived in Phoenix. The woman's parents had split their land between their two children, Bobby Lopez, who was a rug dealer in Albuquerque, and his sister Lupe Lopez. Lupe married a man in real estate, and they moved to Phoenix. To Lupe the land was not important. Her life was in Phoenix, and she did not plan to return to Maravilla ever again. She would prefer to vacation in Cancún or Paris or Venice. Lupe wanted to put the hard work of farming behind her forever. She was not the farming type. So she put her portion of the land up for sale and convinced her brother to let her sell the house too.

In Maravilla, selling land out of the family was almost against the law. It might be okay to sell land to someone across the valley, especially if they were related in some way. But to sell to an outsider, a total stranger unknown to anyone in the village, and one with an odd sort of name too, was beyond the pale. So the men of Maravilla spit on the ground and cursed Lupe Lopez for selling out. The women wondered out loud why this newcomer, this Jacobo Epstein, wanted to live in Maravilla where he had no friends, no relatives and no job. They didn't know that Jake was a writer from New York who was looking for a quiet, peaceful place to write, nor that he had authored several science fiction novels, paying him too meager an amount to live comfortably in Manhattan or Brooklyn, but enough to live tranquilly in Maravilla, New Mexico.

Crystal, at the post office, noticed that the new arrival received formal mail addressed to Jacobo Epstein, and casual mail addressed to Jake. Crystal wondered: *Jacobo was a time-honored Spanish name (if a bit of a fossil), but what was Epstein?* After a little research she learned that during the last millennium, millions of Spanish Jews ran from the sadistic cruelty of the Inquisition like raccoons run from a hound dog. Some of them retained their Spanish identity as well as their Judaism. Jake's family had originally fled to the Netherlands and centuries later to the New World. By then they had lost their Spanish customs, except for certain family names and special foods.

Jake got a cautious reception from his neighbors. The locals were friendly and polite, they smiled and said hello at the post office, but they did not invite Jake into their lives.

It was early April when Jake moved into his house. The trees were turning green, irises were pushing up through last year's dead leaves, and the forsythia was blooming bright yellow next to purple lilacs. Jake changed his schedule dramatically. Now he did most of his writing during the daytime. He got up with the sun, had coffee on the front steps and enjoyed the birds calling to one another before he sat down to write.

Bobby Lopez had kept his half of the land. He leased it to Horacio Mendoza, who grazed his cattle on it. In June, Horacio took his cows up to the mountains, to government lands where the cattle were allowed to roam freely. All summer Horacio irrigated the pasture and let the grasses set their seed before cutting it in July and again in September.

In the fall, when the aspens turned to gold in the mountains, and the chamisa bloomed in yellow splendor, Horacio and his helpers rounded up all the loose cattle and brought them back to Bobby's fields. In the wintertime Horacio fed last summer's hay to his cows. Each morning bundled up against the cold, he wrestled two bales of hay onto the back of his old flatbed truck. Even in the coldest weather, the red truck reliably roared to life. Horacio honked his horn a few times as he approached the pasture, and the cows looked up at the sound. They began to trudge to the center of the field where Horacio always fed them; the cows mooed with anticipation, glad to have something fresh to chew on. The day was often bright with sunlight, the sky clear and blue; the light sparkled on the snow with countless tiny rainbows. Horacio stood on the back of his red truck, leaning on his pitchfork, watching his cows eat the green hay.

But in April, when he had just moved into his little house, Jake had not yet had the opportunity to observe Horacio's yearly cycle. He sat on his porch watching Horacio feed his cows. After a few weeks, Jake got up and put on his boots and jacket. He walked down the dirt road, recently turned to mud from a spring storm, ducked through the fence, and strolled out to Horacio's truck, giving the cattle a wide berth.

"Hey, Horacio," Jake yelled. "Wanna come in for a cup of coffee?"

Horacio said, "Okay. What's it gonna cost me?"

"This one's on the house. I'll go put on the coffeepot."

Horacio finished up with his cows, then drove up to Jake's. The pungent aroma of coffee floated through the house.

"Mmmm. That smells good," said Horacio.

They drank coffee sitting by the warm woodstove, and Horacio told Jake what it was like when he was growing up, eighty-some years ago: plowing the fields with horses, grinding their own flour, raking and bundling the hay by hand before the invention of the miraculous baler. He had always lived in Maravilla; he had been to Santa Fe a few times and once to Albuquerque.

"We live in paradise," contended Horacio. "Why go anywhere else?"

This was the beginning of a friendship beween Jake and Horacio. Once a week or so, Horacio would stop by to tell stories and have a cup of coffee. He loved Jake's coffee. Jake told stories too—about New York City, where people lived high above the ground and traveled beneath it— but Horacio was skeptical of everything Jake said. "You make up stories for a living," Horacio pointed out. "Why should I believe you?"

That spring Jake had a disagreement with Horacio regarding gophers. Farmers in northern New Mexico have persistent problems with gophers, a subterranean dwelling rodent whose only redeeming quality is that they provide food for coyotes, which is not exactly high praise. Jake planted a garden and had trouble with gophers eating his root crops, so he trapped as many as he could. He knew it was not a quick and easy death for the gopher. When the steel cord snaps shut around his neck or chest, it must hurt, although Jake wondered why he never heard a gopher cry out in pain. But as gophers created so much damage, it was hard for Jake to have compassion for them. Over a few months he became a hardened killer when it came to rodents in his garden. He killed them without remorse, and was gravely disappointed when the gophers thwarted his effort to trap them. It only made him more determined, and he set more traps.

Likewise, Horacio had no sympathy for the gophers, yet he didn't see any point in trying to trap them. He considered it a waste of time. He claimed that he had tried for years to chase the varmints off his land, but he found it impossible to eradicate them. After failing, season after season, to defeat them in battle, the gophers won. Horatio raised the white flag. He gave up. He resigned himself to living with the tunnel rats. "Damn gophers," he would say philosophically, "Can't do nothing about them."

Now, whenever Horacio Mendoza irrigated his alfalfa—growing on the field above Jake's—a significant amount of water would run off his field onto Jake's garden and threatened to flood his house. Some of the water came over the top with the natural slope of the land, but most of it came through gopher tunnels. In mid-summer, Jake's garden looked terrible. The plants were stunted and anemic. Jake thought about it and concluded that the excess water from Horacio's field was ruining his garden, causing it to rot in the ground.

Jake had planted his garden as a meditation, as a spiritual practice that would put him in touch with Nature, maybe even with God. The planting and hoeing and weeding also provided a needed balance to his writing, for which he sat at a computer for hours on end. But now Horacio's leaky field was putting his garden in jeopardy, and Jake was feeling anger toward Horacio and even toward God himself. If God giveth and taketh away, he fumed, He should damn well take the gophers away. Short of that, he wanted Horacio to control his own water.

Jake went to see the mayordomo, Juan Mendoza. At age 76, Juan Mendoza had been mayordomo of the Maravilla ditch for twenty years. He felt the weight of responsibility on his back: people expected the water to come and if it didn't it was the mayordomo's fault. If there was a blockage upstream, people complained to the mayordomo. If there was no rain, people screamed for water to be pumped from the lake. On the other hand, Juan decided who would get the water, and when, and for how long. It all had to balance out. People with gardens were in the front of the line because they didn't need much water. Pastureland was last because it needed the most. In between were cottage industries of apples or red chile, grown by farmers who sold their produce at a roadside stand or the Farmer's Market, or those who bartered food for labor. Of course, it was easy for someone to steal the water when it was not his turn to irrigate. Then the mayordomo would get angry phone calls from down-stream users.

So Jake outlined his problem to Juan.

"Did you talk to Horacio about it?" he wanted to know. Horacio, 80 years old but still working hard every day, was Juan's older brother. They lived next door to each other. Jake said that, yes, he had already talked to Horacio about it but that Horacio had just shrugged it off, blaming it all on the gophers. "Those damn gophers," he had said to Jake, as they stood ankle deep in water and mud. "Can't do nothing about them."

"Did you buy this land through the mail?" asked Juan.

"No," Jake replied. He had seen it, walked it, checked it out in the usual way one inspects a property. But Maravilla is an unusual sort of place.

"Didn't you see the *acequia*?" asked Juan, implying that Jake should have noticed the irrigation ditch passing through his property.

"I saw it, but I didn't know what it was," Jake answered honestly. "I thought it was a stream."

"*Ay, cabrón!*" exclaimed Juan, who had grown up in the *acequia*-based farming culture of northern New Mexico. Having lived there all his life, he knew everything there is to know about *acequias*—everything, that is, except that 99.9% of the country has no idea what an *acequia* is. *Acequias* are as central to this lifestyle as subways are to a New Yorker. To Juan, Jake's total ignorance was hard to understand.

Jake wanted to get back to his problem. "Not only does Horacio's water flood my garden and threaten my house, it also floods the road and turns it to mud. I can't even get out of my driveway."

"You need a truck out here," said Juan. "That little car of yours is for city streets."

Juan was not being helpful. "Is there nothing you can do?" asked Jake.

Juan shrugged. "What do you suggest?"

Jake had thought about this. "How about we use a backhoe to dig a trench around Horacio's field and fill it with rock so as to disrupt all the gopher tunnels. Then the excess water will drain slowly through the rocks instead of onto my land and the road."

"And who will pay for this work?"

"I'll split it with Horacio."

Juan thought about it. "'*ueno*, I will ask him," he said at last.

When Juan presented the idea, Horacio flew into a rage.

"You want me to dig a trench around my own field?"

"It's all for the best, *hermano*. The road won't get muddy when you irrigate."

"But look at all the land I will lose to that trench. He should pay me for the loss of property."

"It's not even yours, Horacio. It belongs to Bobby Lopez."

Horacio grumbled but approved the plan, and Jake hired a backhoe operator to do the work. Of course it was not as straightforward as Jake would have liked. Alongside the road, there were two large sinkholes, perhaps ten feet deep and ten feet across. The two sinkholes were not exactly empty. They were filled with debris of all sorts that had to be removed before the trenching could begin. The backhoe operator took to the task with relish. First he pulled out huge piles of brush: dead branches, stumps and one entire cottonwood tree that had fallen over when the earth beneath it collapsed into the ever-widening sinkhole. Beneath the brush was a collection of trash that had been dumped there over a period of many years—shoes, car tires, a dozen plastic five-gallon buckets, several dozen beer bottles, a muffler assembly, all sizes of cans, a few paperback books, leaky garden hoses, a child's highchair, an auto bumper, barbed wire, and a few slabs of concrete. This half-buried trash had not provided good fill for the sinkholes. On the contrary, it created empty nooks and crannies where gophers could thrive and water could easily drain. Once the debris had been excavated, the backhoe operator easily dug the trench and filled it with rock.

In this way, for a few weeks, Horacio's excess irrigation water ran into the trench and largely stayed off of Jake's field. Jake was smug about it. "You see, Horacio, all it takes is a little ingenuity."

Horacio's face remained stern as a statue. "Just wait," he said. Soon the gophers were busy digging new tunnels under the trench. It wasn't long until they had dug all the way through to Jake's side of the trench. Then water once again found its way to Jake's land through the new maze of underground gopher tunnels. "I told you," Horacio said to Jake. "Damn gophers. Can't do nothing about them!"

Chapter II, in which Tai-Keiko comes upon a slimy pyramid in a forest of ferns.

It was dark when Tai-Keiko awoke. The air smelled sweet—too sweet to be enticing or even pleasant. A warm breeze carried the scent. Tai-Keiko could hear wind chimes jingling in the distance. At first she could not remember where she was—or where she had been when she had fallen asleep. As the fog in her brain cleared, the events of the day before returned to her. The emergency landing, the deserted city, the dogs, the crone . . . Yet she was not where she had been. She had fallen asleep in the crone's room, under a warm blanket, and now she was somewhere else: outside on a grassy patch of land, surrounded by fern-like plants of all sizes and colors—shades of green, blue, orange and white.

Beside her sat her spacecraft. Tai-Keiko climbed into the pilot's seat and flipped the ignition switch. The craft immediately sprang to life with a gentle hum. Then she tested the systems and controls. Gravity generator, check. Resonance coil, check. Transducer, check. Was this a dream? A hallucination? With great anticipation, she punched in the coordinates of her location relative to the Milky Way galaxy only to discover that she was nowhere near Zeton-9. She appeared to be in the Sombrero Galaxy, on an unknown planet some 30 million light years from Earth.

Ignoring for the moment the question of how she got there—with her spacecraft intact, operational and even fueled—Tai-

Keiko turned off the craft, disabled all functions and locked it down. She wanted to find out more about this planet before she left. Still, she was keenly aware of the time. Her prime mission was not planet exploration. Her prime mission was delivering the Formula to Commander Fallback on Zeton-9. If she failed, well . . . the grasp of the Krossarians would become tighter, the reach longer, the foot on the neck heavier.

The warm air made Tai-Keiko wonder how it maintained its heat when there appeared to be no sun. Perhaps it radiated out from the center of the planet. According to her mobile transducer, the atmosphere was oxygen-rich yet, apart from the ferns, there were few plants to be seen and no trees at all. After another few minutes, the sweet smell became cloying, then foul, as if on the verge of decay. Maybe this was the price of having no natural light. Tai-Keiko preferred planets with a sun or two to light the world—like her home planet, Earth. Luckily, with her vimax lenses, she could see well in the dark.

Looking around, Tai-Keiko discovered a path that led her through a forest of ferns. Other less familiar plants grew alongside the ferns, but most of them appeared to be dying. In fact, some plants displayed an unusually brief life cycle, pushing their way out of the ground, growing two or three feet within a matter of minutes, and then slumping and falling to the ground, slimy with death. In fact, Tai-Keiko noticed that the ground beside the path was covered with putrid black slime. Only the ferns seemed to thrive.

Eventually, Tai-Keiko arrived at a formidable stone structure, similar in size and shape to a Mayan temple. She walked around the pyramid. Each side had a stairway ascending to the top. She found but one entrance, a massive opening 10 steps from the bottom. Tai-Keiko tried to climb the steep and narrow stairs, but they were covered with the same slippery coating as the dead plants were, preventing her from climbing more than three steps up before sliding back to the ground. The slimy goo oozed out of the cracks where plants were growing and dying. At the bottom of the pyramid, the ferns reached for Tai-Keiko's legs and grabbed at her feet, like the hands of a drowning man trying to grasp a life preserver.

To climb up the slimy steps, Tai-Keiko activated her subspace wave reducer. She corrected the eco-orientation system and set it to the proper frequency. Then the transformer cells took effect, and she became a kind of chameleon, moving easily through the goo with her zygodactylous feet.

Tai-Keiko worked her way up the building—scamper-stop, scamper-stop—advancing in bursts, rather than moving in steady, straight lines like a colony of ants. She tried to go full-speed ahead without stopping, but could not. It was scamper-stop or nothing.

Tai-Keiko looked slowly around through her heavily-lidded eyes, each eyeball looking in a different direction. She blinked and resumed her ascent. As she climbed, she felt a thousand suction cups on the bottom of her feet, designed to cling to any surface—in this case, a rough stone facade, slick from the dying vegetation that grew in the cracks of the stone temple.

Coming to the opening, Tai-Keiko peeked over the threshold.

The room was filled with creatures made entirely of bubbles, large and small, bubbles inside of bubbles, double bubbles, chains of bubbles, colored bubbles, iridescent bubbles—all born of the same slick and transparent gel as the dead plants. They talked to each other in a language filled with soft peeps and pops that Tai-Keiko dubbed Bubble Babble. The Bubble folk were about three feet tall and plump. They drifted effortlessly around the room until they bumped into something hard or sharp, popping the bubble babbler and sending a spray of slime across the room.

Tai-Keiko's chameleon-like senses detected something good to eat. Insects. They were swarming around the buckets of food scraps sitting behind the kitchen. Tai-Keiko scampered up to a convenient place on the top of the bucket. The bugs swirled around in a buzzing cloud. Tai-Keiko stayed as still as stone, except for her long tongue that she flicked into the must around the garbage pile. It was easy pickings.

Tai-Keiko didn't see the big bubble coming. She had changed her color to blend in with the stone wall, but she couldn't fool the enforcer, who grabbed Tai-Keiko in his stinky, soapy claw-like extrusion and was about to detach her head from her body—perhaps a delicacy on this far-flung planet—but Tai-Keiko slipped from his slick hand and jumped for the steps, hitting the top one and falling, sliding, swirling down the temple steps onto the ground, bruised but free. She wiped off the slime that covered her bulging eyes and spat out the goo that had gotten into her mouth. It had a hideous taste. "Like rotten toads," she thought. It had been years since she had been forced to eat rotten toads, but even now the smell made her gag. Tai-Keiko scampered across the apron encircling the pyramid—slippery with dead flowers—scraping off the gray detritus with the suction cups on her feet.

When she entered the fern forest, Tai-Keiko changed back into her human form and ran for her spacebug. She started it up and left that putrid planet as quickly as she could.

To Be Continued. . .

Chapter Four

According to economists—anonymous cubicle-dwelling, number-crunching, head-scratching government bureaucrats—Maravilla was a pocket of poverty. By almost any measure, its citizens were not well-off: their incomes were low, they lacked medical insurance, many people were on food stamps, blah, blah, blah. But no one could convince Maravillosos that they were poor. True, they didn't have much money, but their families and friends and beloved pets all lived together, mostly in peace, in a place the travel magazines had called "enchanted" and "a hidden gem." It was also a place with more than its share of unusual or unique individuals—some called them loco.

Take Arturo "Archie" Archuleta for example. Born in Maravilla some 35 years ago, he had been a strange boy. He didn't talk until he was five—later he joked that he hadn't had anything to say before then—but due to lack of money and insurance, he had never been clinically tested or diagnosed. Some said he had a touch of autism in him. Others pegged it as Attention Deficit Disorder. Maybe he was just slow-witted—his teachers whispered that he was not the brightest star in the sky—but everyone agreed that he wasn't quite normal upstairs. No one held it against him, though, because Archie was friendly and harmless—even helpful if anyone asked him to be.

Archie had always been fascinated by fire. As a child, when someone was burning brush, Archie wouldn't leave the pile before the last flame flickered off into smoke. And even then, he'd hang around watching the coals glow until the orange had turned gray. Among his crayons, the red, orange and yellow ones were worn down to stubs. The green ones were nearly untouched, except for scenes of forest fires or blazing Martian invasions. All of Maravilla was worried that Archie's interest in fire would become an interest in arson.

But in Maravilla, miracles could happen. For Archie it happened in the metal shop at school. In the classroom Archie could not sit still or pay attention—forget about taking a standardized test. Early on, his teachers labeled him as a troublemaker who disrupted class and disobeyed instructions. But when he was old enough for metal shop, where the forge glowed orange and the flames turned white with heat, he was welded to his seat. Suddenly, he could calm down and focus.

The teacher in metal shop was a 60-year-old former blacksmith and fix-it man who had turned to teaching as his metalsmithing business declined. The teacher came from a dying breed of master craftsmen, and he was the miracle in Archie's life. Many kids were curious about metalwork, but to Archie it became an obsession. He learned everything he could and asked for more. He started off learning how to bank the coals, how to heat a metal rod, how to hammer it and how to work it when it softened. Over time he became expert with the tongs and hammer, learning to bend the metal to his will, to flatten it, twist it, taper it. Eventually he made ornate chairs, picture frames, gates and candleholders. Archie enjoyed making these utilitarian objects, but what he liked best was making abstract sculptures out of metal scraps. These pieces were partially forged and partially welded, made of washers and wire and pipe and metal rods, gears and worn-out spark plugs, chrome strips from old cars, chains and railroad spikes—whatever he could find—all connected together into unusual and startling shapes. His pieces were all sizes, from whimsical belt buckles to tabletop sculptures to large pieces for the garden, each one different, similar only in their extravagant ornamentation.

Archie sold his quirky sculptures to local craft shops, displayed alongside more traditional items such as blankets and woodcarvings.

Some people said it was art. Others couldn't see the point. In their eyes, Archie's sculptures were a meaningless mass of metal, the work of an oddball kook, junk piled onto junk, signifying nothing.

Archie didn't care what people said. He kept on doing his thing, nimbly able to ignore the criticism and sidelong whispers, although no one could ignore the innocent shout of a child: "Hey, this is all just a buncha junk!"

Archie just laughed. When it came to scrap metal, nothing abraded his enthusiasm or good humor. Wherever he went, he picked up scrap metal of all kinds, from a car's chrome bumper to the rustiest nut or screw. As years went by, people in Maravilla began picking up pieces of scrap metal themselves and saving them for Archie. Archie received it all with a democratic sense of equality, just as happy with the screw as the bumper. He would take the gifts home, where everything was sorted and stored as neatly as socks. He had bins of bolts and a sink full of screws; he had racks of rods and drawers of derelict bicycle parts. He had all gauges of wire, round, square and braided. He had springs and spikes and pails of nails. From these materials, he fashioned the sculptures that people found artful or awful.

Despite his enthusiasm for metalwork, Archie had a dangerous flaw that dulled his imagination: he drank too much. More often than not, he held a can of beer. A six-pack was rarely in sight, so it was widely assumed that Archie had stashed cans of beer in various places around Maravilla so he was never far away from a drink. He frequently had a pint of whiskey in his hip pocket too.

Archie didn't make a living from his junk sculptures. He worked as a hired hand for Pete Gonzales, who was the largest landowner in Maravilla. Pete kept horses and sheep, grew alfalfa and chiles, and paid a fair wage. He pastured about twenty head of cattle in the cold weather months, and it was Archie who scuffed his way down the road every winter morning to feed hay to Pete's cows. A locked trailer of hay stood at the far end of the pasture, and Archie took out a few bales, broke them apart and scattered them amongst the cows. After he had scraped the shit off his boots (for it was impossible to avoid the cow dung) he walked a mile or so to Julio's barberia, where he could be sure to find hot coffee and sweet rolls. Archie would sweep up the hair clippings that had accumulated so far that day. He brushed off the barber's tools and got clean towels for Julio.

Eventually he would head on home to find out what Pete had in store for him that day. Usually it was along the lines of chopping wood, pulling weeds and pruning back thickets of willow. Archie worked steadily, if slowly, for two hours. After a baloney and cheese sandwich, and another beer, he took a nap.

Archie lived in a small trailer on the back of Pete's property in a remote and almost secret location. In contrast to his neat and orderly collection of scrap metal, the rest of Archie's place was a mess. Dirty clothes carpeted the floor. A half-cleaned flywheel took up most of a battered coffee table. The sink was full of encrusted dishes that had overflowed to the all-weather sofa sitting outside the front door of the trailer home. Strewn around the ground outside were a pair of old slippers, an empty dog food bowl, a bicycle missing its front tire, some dirty jeans, an old girlie magazine and an aluminum trash can overflowing with crushed beer cans. The yard was pure dirt, with no grass and not even a weed in sight. Twenty feet away was a barn that had been abandoned halfway through its construction. It had a roof but no sides. This open-air barn was where Archie had set up his forge, with the smokestack going up through the metal roof. A hammer and anvil waited next to the forge. This was the only place where Archie felt completely comfortable.

Archie was 35, but he looked much older. His rough-hewn lifestyle had taken its toll on his body as the bumps, bruises, cuts and broken bones piled up. His appearance was scraggly and careless. He wore the same clothes every day, regardless of the season: dark hoodie and dirty jeans, work boots and a sweat-stained Lobos baseball cap. His fingernails were rimmed with black soot. Archie had a friendly face with a lopsided smile that put people at ease. Pete left him alone as long as he did his work. Once in a while Pete would insist that Archie clean up his pigsty of a home, and Archie would do that, too. Pete did not allow Archie to run any farm equipment for fear of damage to one or the other. Archie was good with the cows, though. He was not afraid of them and, scrawny as he was, he pushed the massive beasts around like big, dumb dogs.

One day when Archie woke up from his nap, he went looking for Pete but didn't find him anywhere. He had an impulse to take a walk. Archie rarely followed the roads in Maravilla. He preferred to go cross-country, hiking through pastures and orchards, climbing over fences or following a dry *acequia*. He decided to stop at Maravilla Blessings to see if they had sold any of his one-of-a-kind scrap metal crosses.

Located near the Cross of Holy Air Catholic Church, Maravilla Blessings offered a remarkable variety of religious folk art with silver santos, exquisite woodcarving, fine tin work, and milagros for all possible ailments. The display cases were carefully laid out so that every item was dignified with its own space. Archie's unique crosses hung on the wall alongside other more conventional crosses.

Pilar Medina ran the store from her wheelchair behind the counter, and nothing escaped her watchful eyes, constantly surveying her domain. She made sure the items were neatly shown, fully stocked, correctly priced and labeled. She pointed with her cane to indicate where to find a certain item. "Second drawer down on the left" or "Look in the red box by the phone." Despite her large inventory, she knew each piece intimately: who made it, how she got it, how much it cost, how well it sold. She scrutinized every bill the store received. "Paul Padilla overcharged us for these icons," she said, looking through a shipment and its invoice. "He promised them at $14.00 apiece and charged us $15.00."

"I'm sure it was just a mistake, Mama," said her daughter Paloma. "I'll talk to him." Paloma attended classes at the community college and worked at the store a few hours a day, full-time in the summer.

Pilar shifted her large bulk in the wheelchair. "Wasn't there supposed to be some ornamental crosses in that shipment?" she asked.

"You said to wait until the price came down."

"*De verdad*. Padilla is too expensive. Archie Archuleta could make them for half the price. His crosses are kind of strange, but customers like them."

"Should I order some from Archie?"

"Yes, let's get . . ."

Just then Archie walked into the store.

"*Hablando del rey de Roma,*" Pilar said.

"Here I am!" Archie said, grinning. "How are you Paloma? Pilar?"

"Guess what, Archie," Paloma said. "We've sold all your crosses and Mama wants you to make us some more of them."

"*Qué bueno*. How many?" Archie asked.

"A dozen," said Pilar.

"A dozen?" Archie repeated. "Nah, that is too much work. How about four?"

"Archie, Archie, Archie," said Pilar shaking her head. "*Andar buscando trabajo pidiendo á Dios no encontrarlo.*"

Archie shrugged and looked away. He knew it was true: he looked for work half-heartedly, hoping to God not to find any.

"Six then," said Pilar.

"Okay. I will make you six," said Archie, shamed into consent. "Twenty-five dollars each. There's only one problem."

"What's that?"

"I need an advance," he said. "For materials."

Pilar snorted. "Hah! What materials? More junk metal? You mean you need money for more booze."

Again Archie shrugged and looked away.

Paloma gave him twenty-five dollars and made him sign a receipt for it.

"I'll give you a twenty-dollar bonus if you finish in a week," said Pilar.

"You can count on me," said Archie in a tone that begged forgiveness even though he had not yet failed.

Back home, Archie swept out the abandoned half-barn and started up the coals in the hearth. By and by the coals got red hot. He laid out some pieces of metal on a bench. He sipped on a beer while he looked for combinations that would make interesting crosses. Over the next few days, using the forge and his acetylene torch, working on an anvil, he twisted and cut and bent and hammered the metal scraps into the shapes he wanted and then welded them together, giving him five unique crosses. Their only common feature was a bead of copper that defined the crosses. Copper was expensive, so Archie had stolen some from the supply yard at the telephone company.

"These are very nice," said Pilar when Archie presented them to her. "But there are only five of them. You said you'd make six."

"No, I'm sure it was five, with a $25 bonus for getting them done on time."

"You had to make six to get the bonus."

"Señora Pilar, you are such a slave driver! I need a break for a few days."

"Oh, Archie," said Pilar, shaking her head. *"La pereza es llave de la pobreza."*

"Who you calling lazy? I ain't rich, but I ain't lazy neither."

"Five crosses, no bonus."

"All right then. Just pay me for these. Thirty dollars each."

"Twenty-five was the price."

"Thirty is a fair price, *qué no?*"

"Maybe, but it's not the price we agreed on."

"I always give you my best price, Pilar. Where's your sense of loyalty?"

"What's loyalty got to do with it, Arturo Archuleta?" Pilar was one of the few people who remembered Archie's given name. "If you could get thirty bucks apiece somewhere else, you would, and you know it. So don't give me that loyalty crap. Now go make me some more crosses."

With that Pilar paid Archie what she owned him, $100, and shooed him out the door with her canes.

Chapter Five

Jake gradually got to know his way around the meandering roads of Maravilla. He became friendly with his neighbors and bantered with Crystal at the post office. Like everyone else, he frequented Victor Sandoval's general store. "The General," as it was known, carried an astonishing variety of goods, from tools to teapots. Victor Sandoval, a cheerful widow in his eighties, had been a career Army officer, and he shared the nickname of The General with his store. Probably the most common phrase among residents of Maravilla was, "Maybe The General has it," and chances were he did.

Jake got his hair cut at Julio's *barberia*, where he listened quietly to the gossip, trying to separate the truth from the jokes—a task made harder by the fact that half of the talk was in Spanish. A bar on the edge of town—Red's Blue Chile Tavern—piqued his curiosity, yet it seemed forbidding for strangers or newcomers, and he was reluctant to go in.

And that was about it. Maravilla had no bank, no gas station, no library and, above all, no grocer. The General carried the basics—milk, eggs, bread and canned goods—but for fruit, vegetables and meat, folks had to make a trek to San Ramón or Santa Fe.

One sunny afternoon, Jake got up his nerve and stopped at the Blue Chile Tavern on his way home from the post office. The door was open, but the screen door was locked. He knocked. A man came to the door.

"You open?" asked Jake.

"Sure, why not?" said the man, unlocking the door.

Jake walked in and let his eyes adjust to the dim light. He was the only customer.

"How're you doing today?" said Jake.

"Can't complain. No one would listen if I did. How 'bout you?"

"Everything would be perfect if I could get a cold beer."

"No problem there," said the bartender. "Light or not?" He grabbed a plastic cup and sauntered over to the only two taps that were available.

Jake was accustomed to a choice of a dozen or more beers, from local artisan brews to exotic beers from Europe or Asia. "Not," he said.

The tavern was small, and seemed smaller than it actually was because of a full-sized pool table that sat in the middle of the room. There was also a large juke box with mostly Mexican music on it and a few dated American pop hits: Chavela Vargas to Madonna to Los Lobos. Behind the juke box was a wool blanket featuring a fading shot of the Beatles, circa 1965. The mirror facing the bar was almost obscured by memorabilia: photos, postcards, yellowed newspaper clippings, out-of-date nudie calendars, and other souvenirs. A deer's head was mounted at one end of the room, a five-point buck, beads and feathers draped over its horns. A maroon sombrero decorated with gold sequins hung next to the deer. Everything was covered in a film of dust and grime because everything had been there a very, very long time.

"Does the jukebox work?" asked Jake.

"That depends on whether you push the right buttons. You gotta take your chances with that one. It's like a slot machine."

Jake noticed several old knives and swords hanging in one corner behind the bar. Jake pointed to them. "In case you have trouble with a customer?" he asked.

"No, I collect knives. If I need protection, I got a gun under the bar. You don't live around here, do you?"

"Now I do, yeah. I moved here a few months ago."

"From where?"

"New York City."

"No kidding? You a Knicks fan?"

"Not really. Baseball's my game."

"Around here it's basketball. Nobody gives a shit about baseball."
Jake sipped his beer. "I'm Jake Epstein," he said.

"Red Baca." Benny Baca, Red's father, had had dark features, but he had married an Anglo with flaming red hair and freckles. Red had light brown skin with curly red hair; his face was a Milky Way of freckles.

They shook hands.

"Is this your bar?"

Red nodded. "My grandfather built it in 1937. He handed it down to my father, and now it's mine. I didn't want it when I was younger, but then I put in twenty-five years at a desk job for the state." He shrugged at the obvious conclusion. "Now I got a pension, and a bar."

Jake looked around at the jumble of junk, the array of artifacts, the mélange of materials covering every shelf and wall and nook, a willy-nilly collection of stuff.

"You got a lot of history here, Red. A lot of memories. You should call it the Blue Chile Tavern and Museum."

"Ain't that the truth! Take this here." He freed a dollar bill from its thumbtack and pointed to an inscription on the bill. "See that? It's signed by Robert Redford." He held it out so Jake could see. "He came by once with a crew looking at sites for a movie he was making. He liked the bar, but it wasn't quite what he wanted. Anyway, I asked him to sign this dollar bill, and he did. Look. It says, 'To Red. Nice bar! Bob.' That's what they call him. Bob, not Robert." He pinned the dollar bill back on the wall.

"Or how 'bout this one?" Red plucked off a black-and-white photo of a band fronted by an accordion player. "Know who this is? Flaco Jimenez. The grandfather of *norteño* music. He played here with his band in . . ." Red paused to check the back of the photo. "1959. August 7, 1959."

"In here?" asked Jake, surprised. "Where'd you put him?"

"Oh. I have a dance hall in back," said Red. "Come on, I'll show you." Out the back door and across a small courtyard was another building. Inside was mostly empty, except for some chairs and round tables around the perimeter. There was a wooden floor and a stage about three feet off the ground. "This is where Flaco played. We still have dances in here, too. Every Saturday night."

"Cool. I'll have to come by sometime."

When they returned to the tavern, a man was sitting at the bar.

"What's up, Archie?" Red asked. He poured a beer for Archie without asking.

"Not much, Bro. You?"

"This here's Jake," Red said. "A new arrival to Maravilla from New York City."

"Cool," Archie said extending his hand. "I'm Archie."

"If you ever need any metal work done, Archie's your man," Red said.

"Good to know," Jake said.

After a few more pleasantries, Jake decided to leave. He bumped fists with Red and Archie and walked back into the blinding light.

Chapter Six

The meeting to discuss the post office took place on a clear Saturday afternoon in May. The cottonwood trees had new leaves, light green sprouts that shimmered in the breeze and radiated a glorious flickering light. The meeting was set for 3:00, and by then Red's parking lot was jammed. Cars and trucks were parked on the narrow shoulders of the road for a quarter mile in each direction. Red had twenty folding chairs reserved for the *ancianos*. Everyone else stood in tight knots talking loudly. Pilar pushed herself out of her wheelchair and mounted the bandstand, leaning on her canes, and whacked a table for attention. The talking subsided. Jake took a chair in the back. He felt conspicuous as he looked around at a sea of unfamiliar faces—mostly browner than his pasty white skin.

"You all know why we're here today," said Pilar. "We want to keep the post office open." This pronouncement was greeted by cheers and applause. "The question is—how do we do this? It is easy to fight each other, but hard to fight the government." Laughter, and someone shouting, "You got that right!"

"For starters," Pilar continued, "I think we need a petition, signed by everyone in Maravilla, asking the government to keep our post office open. I've got a pile of petition forms here, so be sure to sign one before you leave today, and take some with you, too. But a petition is probably not enough. So I am asking for suggestions, and Paloma is going to write them down. Then we will see."

There was a short silence before someone yelled out, "Let's mail dead fish to the postmaster!"

"Let's burn down the post office in San Ramón," said Archie, who was on his seventh beer of the day.

"Let's kidnap Crystal and only release her when they promise to leave our post office alone," though nobody held any ill will against Crystal, the postmistress for Maravilla. They sympathized with her and said they were sorry she might have to leave. Crystal was pretty sure she'd be laid off, although no one had said so. Maybe she'd be forced to take early retirement.

"Look, folks!" Pilar called out over the laughter and jokes. "This is serious! This is life or death! We've lived together for 300 years, side by side, one generation after another. We need to come together over this issue. We don't have our own village government because we're split into two counties. We need a post office to prove our existence. Without a post office, no one will have an address in Maravilla. No address, no Maravilla. We would become part of state history. End of chapter. Close the book!"

Pilar was out of breath after her tirade. She leaned on the table, looking as fierce as a Conquistador. Her nose pulsed as if steam were blasting out of her nostrils.

It was quiet in the hall. Someone coughed.

People looked around the room. Many looked expectantly at Pete Gonzales, a former lawyer who owned more land in Maravilla than anyone else. Others eyed Horacio and Juan Mendoza, two well-respected residents of Maravilla. Juan shrugged his shoulders.

"We all agree with you, Pilar, but we ain't got a good goddamn what to do."

"Señora Pilar," came a voice buried in the middle of the mob. "I have an idea." A small arm waved above the crowd. It was attached to Sylvia da Silva, Paloma's best friend.

"Come up here, Sylvia," said Pilar.

Sylvia wiggled her way through the bodies to the front of the room.

"What is your idea?" asked Pilar. The mob was quiet and strained to hear every word.

"We could declare our independence," said Sylvia in a mumbled whisper.

"Speak up, Sylvia! Lift up your head. Now say it again, louder."

"We could declare our independence," Sylvia practically shouted.

The room was silent for a beat, until someone started to laugh. Laughter broke out around the room until everyone was laughing. Tears rolled down the cheeks of some. Juan and Horacio were joking about who would make the better governor. Victor Sandoval was calculating how much he could save if he didn't have to pay state or county taxes. Pete Gonzales sat smiling, shaking his head as if he had seen it all before. Sylvia stood quietly in front of the room with her hands clasped in front of her. Pilar stood stone-faced at her side.

When the laughter finally died away, Pilar said, "Okay. What do you mean, Sylvia?"

"We could form our own county," Sylvia said without hesitation. "Maravilla County."

Now the tone in the room changed. No one laughed. Instead, the room filled with whispered wonder. People leaned over to their neighbors to say softly, "Could we do that? Could we start a new county?"

"The two counties would put up one hell of a fight."

"I'm not sure it's even legal."

"Shouldn't matter to the state. It might even like the idea. There'd be one more county to shoulder the blame when something goes wrong."

"The first thing to do: stop paying county taxes."

Gradually, the voices ballooned in volume as the idea, tethered to the ground, began to rise into the air.

"Folks!" boomed Pilar, "if I could have your attention for a minute." The hubbub subsided and people turned toward the front of the room.

"To form our own county, Maravilla County, is a crazy idea—so crazy it might even work. If it turns out that Maravilla County is a fantasy and falls on its face, we still might be able to generate enough noise and media coverage to put Maravilla on the map and force the blowhards in Washington to leave our post office alone."

"How would we start?" asked someone.

Pilar turned to Sylvia. "We'd start with a Declaration of Independence," said Sylvia, "which says that if a government goes bad, we have the right to abolish it and to institute a new government. We would have to terminate our relationship with both counties." More comments and wisecracks issued from the room.

"That's my daughter," a woman named Alice da Silva said to Father Ignatius, the Spanish priest who was seated beside her, bewildered by the whole scene. "She's in college," Alice added proudly.

"I'll be doggoned," said Father Ignatius. It was a favorite phrase of his that he had picked up from a local farmer. He wasn't entirely sure what it meant, but he found it useful in many different situations.

During the entire meeting, Jake sat quietly in the back, taking it all in. He decided that it was by far the most democratic meeting he had ever been to: a marvel of participation and frank talk. He wanted to speak out some encouraging words, but he felt constrained by his whiteness, his poor Spanish, his newcomer status. But a moment later, when Pilar asked for a show of hands to see how many favored creating their own county, Jake found himself with his hand in the air, along with a hundred other citizens of Maravilla—everyone except Father Ignatius who didn't understand the question.

"Those opposed?" asked Pilar. This time, Father Ignatius' hand shot up, and a grin shone on his face. But his grin vanished when he realized he had made a mistake and quickly retracted his arm.

A few weeks later a certified letter landed in the mail boxes of the Chair of the Rio Grande Board of County Commissioners and the Chair of the Carson County Board of County Commissioners. The letter said:

"When in the course of human events it becomes necessary for one community to dissolve the political bonds which have connected it to others, and to assume among the counties of the state of New Mexico the separate and equal station to which God entitles it, a decent respect to the opinions of all citizens requires that we should declare the causes which impel us to the separation. In Maravilla our garbage pickup is unpredictable or non-existent; police protection is inadequate; roads are not properly maintained; groundwater is polluted due to illegal septic tanks; and the governing counties are not responsive to our complaints.

"We, therefore, as citizens representing Maravilla, do solemnly publish and declare that the area known as Maravilla (from Montoya's Weaving Shop in the west and the Cross of Holy Air Catholic Church in the east, south to State Road 499 and north to the river) shall be a free and independent county, absolved of all allegiance to the two adjacent counties, Rio Grande and Carson, which now govern Maravilla. And for the support of this declaration, with a firm reliance on divine Providence, we mutually pledge to each other our lives, our fortunes and our sacred Honor."

The pages that followed this declaration contained the signatures of hundreds of Maravillosos, well over the "ten percent of registered voters" required by the state constitution.

Later that day, the two chairmen of the two county commissions had a phone conversation.

"Are these people serious?" asked Frank Abeyta of Rio Grande County. "They can't just form their own county. Can they?"

"I don't know," replied Freddie Sanchez of Carson. "I'll have to ask our County Attorney."

"We need to apply some pressure. We should stop trash pick-up immediately," said Frank.

"Carson County don't have trash pick-up. We could stop the sheriff from responding to calls from Maravilla," said Freddie.

"We don't have 9-1-1 in Maravilla. Those funds got cut last year."

"Well, we have to do something. We can't afford to lose all those property taxes."

Meanwhile, Pilar had sent off a petition to the U.S. Post Office with several hundred signatures requesting that the Maravilla post office remain open. An accompanying letter stated that Maravilla was in the process of becoming its own county, and that every county had the right to have its own post office.

Although the initial impetus for this mini revolt was to keep their post office open, the more people talked about being their own county, the more they liked the idea.

"What does the county do for us?" those in Carson County asked. "They don't even pick up the trash. What do we get for our tax money? *Nada*! We can take care of ourselves. We already do!"

To her dismay, Sylvia had discovered one potential problem. "According to the state Constitution," she told Pilar and Paloma, "a county may incorporate if it is smaller than 144 square miles—no problem there. But we have to have a population of 10,000 or more. Maravilla has about half that many."

Pilar thought a moment. "Does it say we need a population of 10,000 *people*?" she asked.

Sylvia consulted the Constitution. "No. Just a population of 10,000 or more."

"Oh, well then, we should qualify. We have 5,000 people, plus we have at least 5,000 dogs, cats and horses. Chickens and sheep too, if it comes to that. We just need to make sure they all have a name. Without a name, a creature is not an individual. It is just an animal. But with a name, it is part of the family."

Whether or not Pilar's logic would survive a court challenge, no one knew, but it seemed to be the only solution. Where else would they get another 5,000 individuals? They considered counting dead people, but decided that the dead were not really a part of the population any more. So Maravilla entered an intense period of recording all the non-human individuals in the village. Every household had several pets with names—mostly dogs, cats, horses, some goats and a few milk cows. They drew the line at anonymous livestock that went through life without a name, with only tags in their ears or brands on their flanks. That was Pilar's rule: if it had a name, it counted.

Paloma and Sylvia—The Twins, as they were called—set up a database on a computer and kept track meticulously of every pet in town. People came into the shop with a list of their pets, and one of The Twins entered them into the database by owner's name, species of pet, name of pet, age of pet, and any distinguishing feature. Within a few weeks they had a list of over 5,000 more individuals who lived in Maravilla.

One day, Crystal, the postmistress, received a call from the district supervisor.

"What the hell is going on down there?" he demanded to know.

"People here want to keep their post office open. Didn't you get the petition?"

"Petition? Which petition?" he guffawed. "Yes, I got it. I got petitions from every post office in the district slated for closure. Petitions don't mean a goddamn thing. Everyone wants to keep their post office, but we can't afford it. And what's all this about starting a new county?"

Crystal explained that Maravilla had declared its independence and was establishing its own county. "Doesn't that qualify us for a post office?" she asked.

"Hell if I know. I never heard of starting a new county."

"Well, we're going to need a post office. How else can the assessor's office send out property tax bills? What about county election notices?"

"I suppose we'll have to postpone the closure until this county thing is settled. But don't get too excited. Maravilla is still on the chopping block."

Chapter III, in which Tai-Keiko meets a flizzard

The creatures of planet Hu presented a rainbow of colors and a tessitura of textures. There were scales and feathers and skins, thick and thin. They had teeth and eyes and cross-species hearing capacity. Unknown to Tai-Keiko, they had the ability to recognize aromas and to differentiate between them to an infinitesimal degree. Most of the Hus were smaller than humans—the size of foxes—but there were giants among them as well.

Tai-Keiko put on her Baryon invisibility cloak. It made no difference, though, since most of the Hu Creatures could smell her and knew precisely where she was. Tai-Keiko was crouching behind a wall of stone that curved along the river, but the Hus could smell right through it. They were amused at Tai-Keiko's attempt to hide, but they winked at each other and ignored her.

The air was clear with a pinkish cast, and it carried a scent reminiscent of clove oil. Two suns shone in the sky, side by side, both of them small but bright.

Tai-Keiko decided that forthrightness was the best policy. Hiding was dangerous, and running away was suspicious. So she removed her Baryon cape, straightened her spine and walked up to a hybrid Hu, one with both reptilian and avian fea-

tures. She bowed deeply. "Greetings, Hu Creature," she said. "I am Tai-Keiko of planet Earth in the Milky Way Galaxy. I am visiting your planet to escape a rogue race of killers called the Krossarians. Perhaps you know of them. I am seeking a way to reach Zeton-9, in the Whirlpool Galaxy. I beg your assistance in my quest."

The feathered lizard flicked its tongue and stared at Tai-Keiko, unblinking. It began to talk, but its voice was garbled and full of static. A stream of blue liquid shot out of its mouth. The flizzard coughed and spat and swallowed noisily. When it spoke again, its voice was rough-edged but quite understandable to Tai-Keiko.

"Welcome, Earthling," it said. "The Whirlpool Galaxy is many light years from here."

"If I can access the sub-space matrix," said Tai-Keiko, "I can disconnect from the space/time continuum just long enough to reach the Whirlpool without self-destructing. Can I obtain sub-space access on your planet?"

"Of course, but you have to sign up for it. It's in high demand here. Where'd you say you're from? Oh, never mind. Let's go get a drink."

"Okay," said Tai-Keiko reluctantly, knowing the urgency of the situation, but trying not to show her impatience at the delay.

"Right this way," said the flizzard. They boarded a punt and floated with the current on the canal. On one side were trees and a carpet of tiny colorful flowers; on the other were buildings shaped like shells of different sizes. On both sides, the Hu Creatures were fluttering, hopping, rolling and slithering over each other like happy puppies.

*Tai-Keiko had arrived at this curious planet only a few mo-
ments before. She had been free-falling through hyperspace,
dodging comets and asteroids. She had lost control of her
spacebug when a buildup of energy in the distortion field
caused her pulse amplifier to freeze. Fortunately, the atmosphere was thick enough to slow her descent, and her landing
was as soft as a pillow.*

*When she landed, Tai-Keiko's universal orientation system
was still operating, and she was able to determine she was on
the planet Hu in the Pinwheel Galaxy. She remembered study-
ing the Hu in school, but her power converter was too weak to
allow her to access any details. "Come to think of it," Tai-Keiko
thought alarmingly, "if I don't find a way to recharge my converter soon, I will lose all my memory. I would not know how to
use my equipment, or even how to speak. I would become as dependent as a baby, and would likely die from exposure to any of
the viruses on the planet."*

*"This place we're going," Tai-Keiko said to the flizzard. "Is
there a power converter charger there?"*

*"Most certainly there is. Whether it is working is another
question entirely. Our technology in that area has not yet recov-
ered from a severe meteor storm we encountered several suns
ago. The physical damage was minimal, but the extreme heat
fried the anti-matter sensors."*

"I hate it when that happens," Tai-Keiko said.

*The flizzard led Tai-Keiko to a busy bar where an unearthly
clamor filled the air. The flizzards spoke in a chaotically musical tongue that consisted of tweets and trills, glissandos and
blats, gurgles and grunts, high squeals and long bass tones
booming underneath. Their appearance was just as varied.*

Some Hu creatures had red scales and blue feathers, others had the opposite. The Hus had feathers and scales of all hues. But Tai-Keiko could not enjoy this friendly species. She was too worried about recharging her power converter.

"Good Hu Creature," she said, "can you tell me where the recharger would be?"

The Hu pointed to the back of the bar. "Try back by the bathrooms," it said. "I'll order our drinks."

Sure enough, Tai-Keiko found an ancient recharger in a corner by the bathrooms. She plugged in her converter and hoped for the best. At first a red light came on, but a moment later it turned to green and began a reassuring hum. Her memory was intact.

Tai-Keiko returned to the bar room and spotted her flizzard friend waving at her from his table. Waiting for her there was a green drink with black spots floating in the liquid.

"This is a local favorite called a Green Spider," said the flizzard. Tai-Keiko took a cautious sip.

"Hmm. Minty," she said. It was better than she had expected. "What are the black spots?"

Just then a blast of sound engulfed the room, and the dance floor filled up. Tai-Keiko's companion grabbed her hand and pulled her into the swirling fray. After 20 minutes of intense, high-energy, non-stop dancing—feathers flying, claws scratching the floor—the music ended abruptly, and everyone returned to their seats.

"Wow, that was energetic," Tai-Keiko said. "I'm breathless."

"You did quite well for an alien," said the flizzard.

"Thank you," Tai-Keiko said. *But she didn't want to dance.*
She was eager to be on her way. "Where is the sign-up for sub-
space access?" she asked the flizzard.

"Oh, well, let's see." It pulled a device from its jacket pock-
et and pushed a few keys on it.

"It looks like there is an open slot this evening. Shall I sign
you up?"

"Yes, please do."

When she had secured a spot, Tai-Keiko thanked her host
for its help, made her excuses, grabbed her recharged power
converter and headed for the door. She walked along the canal,
anxious to resume her journey. But more troubles were in store
for her.

When Tai-Keiko got back to her spacebug, she discovered
that a hit-and-run driver had smashed into her craft. There was
a note on the windshield that read, "Sorry, pal. I was chasing a
stolen buggy when I lost control and crashed into your craft.
For insurance questions, call my agent."

"Arrgh!" Tai-Keiko howled. She ran some system tests and
found that the errant driver had damaged her resonator coil.
Plus, her pulse amplifier was still frozen. How was she going to
make the necessary repairs in time for her appointment to ac-
cess the sub-space matrix?

After a frantic search, Tai-Keiko located a space freight
company that was able to fit her spacebug on its bill of lading
that evening. The clerk said they could tow her buggie to the
next planet up where he knew a good mechanic. With a sigh of
relief, Tai-Keiko curled up next to her craft and fell asleep. As
she slept, herds of wild animals passed by, heavy animals with
masses of muscle and bone. Not one of them stepped on Tai-

Keiko . In the morning, all that was left of them was a dry mus-ty, meaty smell and a dream of body warmth.

To Be Continued. . .

Chapter Seven

Maravilla's shrine, the Cross of Holy Air Catholic Church, was nearly 200 years old and had withstood revolts, rebellions, invasions and wars. It had been built by a wealthy landowner named Aurelio Salazar who claimed that God had told him in a dream that he should build a church in Maravilla because it was a holy place, and its fresh air had healing powers. So, being a True Believer—and being rich—Aurelio Salazar built a church in grand style across the road from his house. The walls were made of adobe, three feet thick; the beams were Ponderosa pine felled in the mountains and dragged down to the valley by a team of mules; the floor was a mosaic of flat rocks pulled from the river, polished by the rushing water. Aurelio Salazar hired only the best craftsmen to build the church, and the best woodworkers to carve the stations of the cross. The crucifix behind the altar was larger than life and vividly portrayed the pain and suffering of the Son of God on the cross, with blood dripping from his side and blood streaming down his face from the crown of thorns stuck onto his head. Jesus' eyes looked so forlorn and miserable that visitors would put an extra dollar in the collection box out of pity for the wretched Savior.

But the most unusual feature of the church—and the reason that Believers from all over the world came to the chapel—was the Cross of Holy Air. In his dream, Aurelio Salazar saw a cross built into a tower where Maravilla's healing air swirled around inside. So behind the sanctuary, Aurelio Salazar built a round tower, 10 feet in diameter and 30 feet high, with one narrow, arched entrance. Inside the tower, facing the archway, a set of small windows outlined the shape of a cross. These windows had no panes but were simply rectangular holes built into the thick adobe walls, open to the outside. The floor of the tower was made of packed earth, and at its center were two shallow indentations where pilgrims could kneel before the windowed cross and breathe deeply of the Holy Air that flowed in through the windows.

For decades the Cross of Holy Air was an obscure religious site, an oddity unknown to the general public. Then, in 1951, a free-lance reporter wrote a story about the cross in the tower and the reputed healing power of its Holy Air. The story was picked up by the wire services, and almost overnight pilgrims in distress began flocking to Maravilla in hopes that its Holy Air would cure their ailments. A few years later, the church had to build a separate room to hold all the crutches, canes and eye patches that had been discarded by pilgrims who claimed to have been healed by the Holy Air. There were also testimonials. It was widely reported that one man had come on his knees from Santa Fe, shouldering a heavy wooden cross, with only his thin pants for protection from the gravel and small pieces of glass that littered the edge of the road. His story—written in simple, crude handwriting on a piece of cardboard torn from a box—had lain on a table in the Tower for years. During the journey, the pilgrim wrote, he prayed constantly for God to heal his son, who had been born with a cleft palate. In another document, penned in flowery purple script, a woman prayed for the soul of her brother, and asked God to return him safely home from the war. Such stories and affirmations covered the heavy wooden tables that lined the walls of the narrow passageway between the chapel and the Tower.

As word spread of the miraculous healing power of the Holy Air in Maravilla, the line to pray in the Tower became longer each day. Even in bad weather, the line of distressed pilgrims stretched down the hill as far as the river. The church, sensing an opportunity to fund its operation, began to sell small vials of Holy Air at five bucks a pop. Sales were so brisk that the church soon expanded its product line to include ornate stoppered bottles in a variety of colors.

In his will, Aurelio Salazar had given the church to the Archdiocese of Santa Fe through a deal he had worked out with the Archbishop. The Catholic hierarchy was miffed because Aurelio had built the church on his own, without consulting the Archdiocese. The Church showed its displeasure over this presumptuous behavior by refusing to assign a permanent priest to the parish. For years an itinerant priest showed up on a burro to say Mass once a month, but then he disappeared the rest of the month. The Archbishop agreed to bring in a full-time priest if Aurelio Salazar, upon his death, would deed his church to the Archdiocese. Shortly before his death, Don Aurelio staged an elaborate ceremony—attended by the Governor of the territory, the Archbishop, a judge and the new priest—during which Aurelio Salazar presented the church keys to the Archbishop. All of Maravilla turned out for the occasion. A photographer ducked under the black hood of his clumsy camera to take pictures for the Santa Fe newspaper. The Archbishop knelt before the Cross of Holy Air and gave his blessing to the church in the name of God and the Vatican. It was a memorable day for the village.

Father Ignatius—the current parish priest—came to Maravilla from Spain because of a clerical error. He was supposed to go to Maravilla, Mexico, but when the paperwork came through, it said Maravilla, *New* Mexico. He protested that he didn't speak any English, but the documents had already passed through the Catholic bureaucracy, contained all the appropriate signatures, and no one was willing to start over. So Father Ignatius went to America.

In his ten years there, he had done his best to visit the sick, console the grieving, counsel the troubled, and minister to the spiritual needs of his small flock. Although he loved his parish, Father Ignatius had a knack for making poor decisions. One year he received money from the Archdiocese to build new toilets for the church. Thinking only of convenience, he placed them right next to the courtyard entrance, and, as a result, the peaceful courtyard was spoiled by the sounds of flushing, and the meditative atmosphere was tainted by the foul odor. Another time, Father Ignatius received money for a new parking lot, which he put near the river, rendering the parking lot useless in the spring when the river flooded for weeks at a time. In an attempt to honor Saint Francis of Assisi, he built a bird roost under the eaves of the church, expecting bluebirds, orange-headed tanagers and yellow-breasted finches to add splashes of color to the church. Instead, a flock of pigeons moved in, and soon pigeon droppings covered the roof, falling in great clumps onto the ground alongside the church, and not infrequently onto the parishioners and pilgrims. So often Fr. Ignatius's good intentions went awry.

Over years of scorching summers and bitter winters, bit by bit, the Cross of Holy Air had begun to show its age. The church looked shabby and shaky. The stucco flaked off, the roof beams began to rot, the white-washed walls and ceiling became gray and dingy from the candle smoke. Father Ignatius appealed to the Archbishop to repair the church, but only received enough money for two portable toilets and a parking lot.

Father Ignatius racked his brain for ways to bring in money so he could repair the church and restore it to its former glory. His bills ate up his meager income. The offering at Sunday mass, the tourist dollars and the Holy Air money were barely enough to pay for the utilities and food. He needed a bigger, fatter purse. He thought of the ordinary ways to raise money: an auction, a fiesta, a bingo tournament, but none of them felt right to him. He even considered charging admission to the Tower, but he knew that the Archbishop would never allow it.

After much prayer, Father Ignatius decided to ask the Salazars for help. After all, their best-known ancestor built the church and gave it to the Archdiocese. He practiced a speech, saying, "In the name of Aurelio Salazar, may his soul rest in peace, would they undertake to repair the church?" The Salazars had not lived in Maravilla for decades. When

Aurelio died, the family stayed in the house for several years, but finally they decided to move to Denver and start a mortuary, the Salazar Family Mortuary. Don Aurelio had left a large estate, more than enough to start a funeral business. One of Aurelio's grandsons, Aurelio III, studied "mortuary science" and learned how to embalm a body, how to dress and make-up the corpse. He learned about hearses, coffin suppliers, floral arrangements, and appropriate musical choices. The Salazar Family Mortuary became a successful business, and the Salazars never thought about Maravilla again—until Father Ignatius called.

Father Ignatius spoke to the latest member of the Salazar clan to run the mortuary, Aurelio V. The priest had a hard time explaining himself to Aurelio V. Even after ten years in America, his English was not good, and Aurelio V had never learned to speak Spanish. Aurelio V had heard the story that his namesake had built a church somewhere in New Mexico, but he knew nothing about his ancestor's dream or the Holy Air. After several minutes of painfully difficult conversation, Aurelio V thought he understood what the priest wanted: The church needed work, and he wanted the Salazars to come to its rescue.

Normally Aurelio V would have sent a few hundred dollars to the priest or he might have dismissed this request entirely. After all, the Salazars had not lived in Maravilla for a hundred years. But Aurelio V was a good businessman, and the idea of holy air intrigued him. In his line of work, holy air might be useful. He told Father Ignatius that he would think about it and get back to him. Aurelio then called his accountant and asked him if the family owned any land or buildings in Maravilla. The accountant discovered that the family had been paying real estate taxes on a house in Maravilla as far back as their records went. This was news to Aurelio V, and he asked his son, Aurelio VI, to make a trip to Maravilla and see what exactly they owned.

Aurelio VI drove down to Santa Fe and went to the tax assessor's office where he looked up their property. According to the tax records, the Salazars owned a large house on a few acres of land in Maravilla. Of course it was the dilapidated family house across the road from the church that, for a reason now lost in the fog of time, was never sold when the Salazars moved away. In Maravilla it was known as "the old Salazar house," but no one knew to whom it belonged. Legend had it that Don Aurelio had been buried with the deed on his chest. In any case, it had been vacant for as long as anyone could remember, used only by squatters and vagrants. A sheriff's deputy made regular stops at the old house and chased off any interlopers. There were stories of ghosts in the house, a *chupacabra* hiding out there, *La Llorona* wailing, rattlesnakes nesting in hollow places in the walls. It was not an inviting place to spend the night. Over time it had fallen into a sad state of disrepair. Its windows were broken, trash was strewn around the dirty floor. The walls had been tagged with graffiti so many times that it looked like abstract art. Whole sections were missing from the roof and rot was creeping into the beams. It was too old ever to have had electricity or running water, so it sat abandoned, home to mice, sparrows and a family of skunks. Father Ignatius had long thought it an eyesore, a disgrace to the church that should be razed.

Aurelio VI reported back to his father, and they discussed their options. Perhaps the Archdiocese would buy it, for the land if not the building. Perhaps a local businessman would buy it and turn it into a bed and breakfast.

"Maybe it's historical," suggested Aurelio V. "Then the state might buy it."

"Maybe we should keep it," said Aurelio VI.

"Why?"

"I don't know. It's nice there. It's our roots."

But Aurelio VI had a secret motive for wanting to keep the house. He was dying to get out of the mortuary business.

Aurelio VI was a fourth generation mortician. His family had been dealing with dead people for a hundred years, and he was sick to death of it. Comforting the bereaved; peddling expensive caskets that would outlive their occupants by centuries; practicing the dark art of embalming; wearing the same somber uniform every day (black suit, white shirt, gray tie): it was all becoming oppressive. The stench of dead flowers, the dreary organ music, the weeping widows . . . He didn't know how much longer he could bear it. What he hated the most was the false sincerity of some mourners—that is, the ones who were there only because their absence would be conspicuous. Aurelio VI could always spot the phonies. They sat on an aisle seat, checked their watches surreptitiously, tapped their feet and made a beeline for the door as soon as the last "Amen" was said.

It was time for him to close the lid on this part of his life and find another profession.

Besides, the funeral business was changing. No longer could you get a police motorcycle crew to escort the funeral procession from the mortuary to the cemetery. Instead of a long line of cars with their lights on, cruising through stoplights, mourners were left to fend for themselves, stopping for red lights, trying hopelessly to keep up. Then there was the new movement towards "green burials" with "eco-friendly funerals" and "biodegradable caskets." These were new terms coined by the "deathcare" industry. It was all really just a throwback to the old way of doing things: burying people in simple wooden coffins with or without embalming fluid in their veins. Aurelio VI could change with the times if he wanted to. But he had no interest in following that path. Then, while he was visiting Maravilla, lightning struck.

Trying to get a feeling for what sort of place Maravilla was, Aurelio VI stopped at some of the local shops. The village relied on the tourist trade, so he found plenty of blankets, baskets, jewelry, religious items, and local art. When he entered Maravilla Blessings he was surrounded by fine religious folk art, but he barely noticed anything but Paloma. She was dressed in a simple white dress, and her black hair cascaded down her back in luxurious curls. She had full lips with a faint trace of a downy moustache on her upper lip. Her eyes were dark and mischievous. Aurelio thought she was the most beautiful woman he had ever seen.

"Can I help you?" Paloma asked. Her radiant smile devastated Aurelio. He felt his face flush and his knees buckle. He had to grab the counter to keep himself from collapsing.

"What are your most popular items?" he stammered.

"Well, our patron saint icons are best-sellers, and the various vials for Holy Air. But I suppose our most popular item is the cross. We have lots of different crosses."

And so they did: crosses large and small, metal and wood, plain and highly decorated. Aurelio carefully examined several crosses while he composed himself. At the same time, he felt the eyes of Pilar sweeping over him like searchlights as he picked out cross necklaces for his mother and his sister, and a few larger crosses for the mortuary viewing room. Not that they needed more crosses. He just wanted an excuse to hang around Paloma. He asked her obvious questions—Are these made by local artisans? What kind of material is this?—to prolong his conversation with her.

Finally, Aurelio's mind went blank and he handed Paloma his credit card. He noticed there were no rings on her long and graceful fingers.

"Where are you from?" she asked.

"I live in Denver, but my ancestors are from here."

Paloma glanced at his credit card. "Salazar?" she asked. "Aurelio Salazar? He was the man who built our church."

"Yes. He was my great-great-great grandfather."

"Oh, my goodness!" Paloma was genuinely astonished. "Mama," she said. "This man is descended from Aurelio Salazar."

"Yes, I heard," said Pilar. "Where have you been all these years?"

"We're in the funeral business. The Salazar Family Mortuary in Denver."

"A good, steady business, *qué no?*" Pilar burst into laughter. "You never run out of customers." Then the phone rang and Pilar became engaged in a conversation about the price of *bultos*.

"Would you have lunch tomorrow . . . with me?" Aurelio asked Paloma in an impulsive lurch of words. "I'd like to know more about you . . . and Maravilla. I don't really know much about my own background. I bet you could give me the big picture."

"You want to get in touch with your roots, is that it?" Paloma asked with a twinkle in her eyes, guessing Aurelio's real reason for the invitation. "You should go talk to Father Ignatius."

"I suppose so. Good idea. He'd probably know something about . . ."

"Yes."

". . . the history of my ancestors, and . . . Did you say 'yes?'"

"Yes."

"You'll have lunch with me?"

"Isn't that what you asked?"

"Yes. Yes. Terrific! And maybe after lunch you could take me on a tour, just a short tour, of the village?"

"Don't push your luck, mister," Paloma said with a mock frown.

"Okay, sorry. Just lunch then. That'll be great. I'm staying at the Maravilla Bed & Breakfast," said Aurelio. "Here's my card with my cell phone number if you need to reach me."

Paloma took his card. "Thanks, but don't expect me to call," she said.

"No? Well, that's fine. I'll just . . ."

"We don't get cell phone service here."

"What? You don't?"

"Most people still use their landline. We live in a techno backwater. We listen to cassettes and watch video tapes."

"Really?" asked Aurelio in astonishment.

"No, not really. Because we don't have TVs."

"What? No. You're just pulling my leg." Paloma smiled mysteriously. Aurelio said, "I'll meet you here at 1:00 *mañana*. Okay?"

"Sure," Paloma said. "Just remember that '*mañana*' doesn't mean 'tomorrow.' It means 'not today.'"

Chapter Eight

The only place to eat in Maravilla was a friendly café called Josie's Diner, as proclaimed by a neon sign in cursive script, mostly red but occasionally flickering green or yellow. It sang with an ample buzz, reminiscent of bees in a flower garden. The electric sign hung on a fence, near a gate leading to a courtyard where patrons could sit on sunny days. The main entrance was off to the left, two steps up. The restaurant sported a *Día de los Muertos* theme featuring skeletons as the main motif. The rooms had solid colored walls—yellow, blue and deep purple—decorated with a mural of white skeletons dancing, driving cars, dealing cards and delivering plates of food. Plastic marigolds, more yellow than egg yolks, framed the windows.

"You should feel right at home here, with all these skeletons," Paloma said. "Is this how your mortuary looks?"

"Pretty close. Except besides skeletons on the walls, we have zombies roaming the rooms."

"Nice touch."

"Day of the Dead, right?" asked Aurelio, appraising the walls. "We always did Halloween, Trick-or-Treat, but my grandfather told me about *Día de los Muertos.* He said all the dead people would come back to life in the form of their skeletons, and I remember wondering how there would be room for all those skeletons. I pictured skeletons all crushed together in a warehouse with a huge pile of skulls in one corner."

Paloma laughed her wonderful throaty chuckle. "Josie used to change her décor for every holiday. You know: Christmas, Valentine's Day, Easter, July 4th, *Día de los Muertos,* Thanksgiving, Christmas. One year she got tired of changing it, so she picked one and stuck with it."

"So it's always Day of the Dead in here?"

"Yeah. Which is weird because *Día de los Muertos* is a Mexican thing, not *norteño.*"

Aurelio raised his eyebrows skeptically. He studied the walls. "Looks like a Grateful Dead thing to me. These skeletons aren't very scary," he observed. "They look like they're having fun."

"Skeletons don't have to be scary," said Paloma.

"Of course they do. Just like ghosts."

"That's different. Ghosts *are* scary. And *chupucabras* are the scariest of all."

"And what might a *chupucabra* be?" Aurelio asked.

"You don't know? It's a terrifying creature—half lizard, half dog—that sucks the blood of goats."

"I see. But do they make good tacos?"

Paloma smiled, enjoying their ridiculous banter.

The stamped tin ceiling looked retro, but was actually part of the original building from the 1930s. Josie Duran and her husband ran the restaurant with the help of a capable crew. They relied on tourist business, but locals ate there too when they were tired of their home cooking. The menu was a smorgasbord of regional cuisine: *enchiladas, huevos rancheros, tamales, fajitas, burritos* and, of course, the green chile bacon cheeseburger.

Josie was a thin and wiry woman who could chat with the customers and keep working at the same time. Her arm muscles were ropy and strong.

"How've you been, hon?" Josie asked Paloma, giving her a kiss on the cheek. "Business been good? We've been busy here."

"Busy is good, right? Josie, I'd like you to meet Aurelio Salazar. He lives in Denver now, but his family used to live here. You know the old Salazar house? His *abuelos* built it and lived there, and then built the church across the road."

"My word!" said Josie. "We got a celebrity in the house. Welcome to Maravilla, and welcome home, too. Let me get you folks a good seat." Josie found them a private nook just off the main room. Aurelio pulled out a chair for Paloma, who was so unaccustomed to such polite behavior that she almost missed the cue, but caught herself just in time.

"Thank you," she said.

"Can I get you something to drink?" asked Josie.

"Would you like a glass of wine, Paloma?" Aurelio asked. It was the first time he had said her name, and he was surprised how much pleasure it gave him.

"On a weekday? No, I have to go back to work. I'll just have iced tea."

"Two ice teas," said Aurelio.

"So," said Paloma after they had ordered. "I don't think you said yesterday why you are in Maravilla, if you don't mind my asking."

Aurelio unwrapped his silverware from the napkin. "Well," he said. "I'll tell you, Paloma, but you have to promise to keep it a secret. I don't want anyone else to know."

"Better not tell me then. The store is the Castle of Gossip, and my mom is the queen."

"Your mother won't know if you don't tell her. This is just between us, okay?"

"Okay," said Paloma warily. "I'm intrigued."

"Father Ignatius has asked us to help fix up the church. He says the church is in bad shape and he can't get any money from the Archdiocese, and that Maravilla is a poor community; and he said, you know, my family's ancestor built that church himself and then gave it to the Archdiocese so that they would bring a priest to Maravilla. And he said the church is important to the people here, and in the name of the Aurelio Salazar family, could we pay for the repairs it needs."

"Oh, my gosh! So you're down here to take a look at the church and see what's wrong with it?"

"Yes, that's half the reason."

"Here you are," said Josie, approaching with two plates. "Chicken *enchiladas* for you, Mr. Salazar, and *tamales* and *posole* for you, Paloma. You didn't order the *posole*, but I know that you like it. Enjoy your meals."

Josie rushed off. The aroma of chile filled the air around them. Aurelio and Paloma inhaled the pungent steam and smiled.

"I never get tired of that smell," Paloma said. "Even when I was a little girl, I remember my mother making a batch of enchiladas or tamales, and the whole house would fill up with this heavenly cloud of chile that almost always made me sneeze. And my eyes would tear up too."

"Now why would you not get tired of something that made you sneeze and cry?" Aurelio teased. "It probably burned your mouth too. Am I right?"

Paloma laughed slowly, a throaty chuckle that made Aurelio think, *I could live with that laugh for the rest of my life.*

"Don't you have special scents in your life?" asked Paloma. "Smells that you could never mistake for anything else?"

"Your perfume?"

It just slipped out unintentionally, but there it was. Paloma looked away, turning red.

Aurelio was in deep now, so he plunged ahead, trying to make the best of it. "Mixed with the chile smell, it's brilliant. We could use it in soaps and air fresheners and chewing gum."

"It will never replace peppermint," Paloma said, rising to the challenge of an awkward moment. Paloma laughed her sexy chuckle, while Aurelio joined in with his hearty guffaw. It was the first time they had laughed together, and it broke the tension between them.

"How's your *posole*?" asked Aurelio. "Josie brought it just for you. I think she's very fond of you."

"Oh, it's good. Josie makes the best *posole*. Here, try a bite." She handed him the bowl.

"Hmm, delicious."

"What's the other half?"

"The other half of what?"

"You said that *half* the reason you came down to Maravilla was to check out the condition of the church."

"Yes."

"What's the other half?"

Aurelio had intended on telling Paloma that his family still owned the old Salazar house, and that he was investigating that too, but now he didn't want to talk about it. It was too serious and too dangerous a topic. Instead, he said, "I wanted to meet the people who live in Maravilla, especially those who live and work around the church. Like you and your mother. I wanted to introduce myself to the store owners who might be affected by the construction." It was all true but not what he had planned to say.

"That's a good idea," said Paloma. "People like to know what's going on."

"So tell me about yourself. Do you work at the store full-time?"

Paloma explained that she was taking courses at the community college and working part-time, but that she planned to attend UNM full-time in the fall, as an education major. She wanted to be a teacher. For the first time, Aurelio realized that Paloma was still very young. Enchanted by her beauty, now he shivered with dread. "Be careful," he told himself.

"When I was growing up," Paloma said, as if to shoot another arrow toward his heart, "I knew that the church had been built by a man named

Aurelio Salazar. In my mind it was eons ago, when dinosaurs roamed the Earth, and I imagined what Aurelio Salazar must have looked like."

"Anything like me?" asked Aurelio.

"Not at all. For one thing he was much older than you. He had a shock of white hair, and a small, stringy goatee. He was a big man, not fat but hefty, you know, and strong-looking. And he wore a white shirt with a bolo tie."

"Definitely not me. I look like a dork in a bolo tie."

In reality, Aurelio VI was a handsome man with delicate features. He was dressed conservatively—in a pressed white shirt—shined shoes and slacks with a razor-sharp crease—and had soft well-manicured hands. His smooth jaw gave meaning to the term "a close shave."

Paloma laughed her throaty laugh. "This is so weird," she said. "Your ancestor is a legend around here, but I never knew exactly who he was. I just made him up in my head."

"I had never even heard of him until Father Ignatius called a few weeks ago. I found a record of the land transfer to the Archdiocese at the County records office. That was in 1888."

"I wish we had pictures."

"Yeah, wouldn't that be great? But I haven't found any."

"What are you going to do?"

I feel a certain responsibility for the church, even though it was built a long time ago, and we haven't lived here for a hundred years. But I need to convince my father to do it." He paused a moment to eat some of the enchiladas and chased it with some iced tea. "Maybe I need to get my father down here in person. I mean, it's a gorgeous place. He'll go nuts for it."

Paloma smiled knowingly.

After lunch, Paloma said, "Now about that tour . . . Are you still interested?"

"Are you kidding? Absolutely!"

They dropped off Aurelio's BMW at the store, trading it for Paloma's 1984 red Ford pick-up truck. They drove down dusty back roads, past orchards and farms and grazing horses. When they hit pavement again, they drove by the elementary school and the post office and stopped at a weaving shop. Inside there were tables of rugs of various sizes, and racks of woven garments. In the back several people were working on large looms. Aurelio bought a dark brown rug, with a design in red, orange and yellow. "I know just the spot for that," he said.

When they got back to the store, Paloma said she would like to show Aurelio one more thing. They walked past the church to the cemetery. Many of the gravesites were decorated with colorful plastic flowers, and some with a crucifix or an American flag. Paloma showed Aurelio his ancestors' graves, including the original Aurelio Salazar, 1821-1889. Aurelio stood silently looking at the headstone. It felt odd to see his own name on the gravestone. He knelt down and traced the letters with his finger.

"My family is buried over here," said Paloma when Aurelio stood up. She led the way to another part of the cemetery where many of the tombstones had the name "Medina" on them.

"What about your mom's family?"

"She's an Aguilar. They're over there, underneath that old cotton-wood."

"Ah, the family tree," Aurelio said, and Paloma laughed. "So on *Día de los Muertos* all these folks are going to come back to life?"

"Just their skeletons," said Paloma, striking a skeletal pose. "The locals will come here to clean and decorate the graves of their ancestors, and maybe leave food for them to eat. They might make some *pan de muerto*."

"Bread of death? Sounds delicious."

They walked slowly back to the store and said goodbye. Aurelio thanked Paloma for the tour. "I'll let you know more about our little secret after I talk to my dad," he said. Just then the breeze shifted direction and a fetid smell filled the air. Aurelio wrinkled his nose. "Is that the *smell* of death?" he asked.

Paloma laughed. "Some people think so," she said. "But we call it *'el aroma de la vida'.*"

"The smell of life? What do you mean?"

"Pacheco's Pig Farm is just down the road," she said, pointing. "When the wind is blowing our direction, you can smell it. Fragrant, isn't it?"

"Indeed it is. Doesn't it scare away the tourists?"

"Some, I suppose. Personally, I think it's a reminder that holy air and smelly air *son el mismo.* They're one and the same."

"So philosophical! I would just pray for the wind to blow the other way."

"Well, sometimes our prayers are answered, and sometimes they're not."

Chapter Nine

Johnny Pacheco's pig farm was about one-quarter mile east of the Cross of Holy Air Catholic Church. The Church owned that quarter mile and kept it neatly groomed all the way to the sturdy six-foot high fence the Church had built along the property line to make sure that Johnny's pigs could not get onto Church property; nor could the pigs be seen from the Church, although a loud squeal could easily be heard in the Church's courtyard, and the loudest squeals even penetrated the thick adobe walls of the Church itself.

A bigger problem than the sound of the pigs was their smell. As long as the breeze was blowing toward the pig farm, away from the Church, the air smelled sweet and clean, the way one would expect holy air to smell. But when the wind shifted to the west, it carried with it a stench that made it difficult to concentrate on prayers or worship. Indeed, some families would determine whether or not they would go to mass depending on which way the wind was blowing. The number of Church members who went to Confession each day was in direct proportion to the course of the wind. Even the most devout parishioners thought twice about going to Confession when the wind was blowing in, holy air or not.

Father Ignatius had tried several things to mitigate the foul odor coming from the pig farm. He had offered to relocate Johnny's pig farm to another spot, complete with a barn, a fence and new feeding troughs, but Johnny liked it where he was. Father Ignatius had hung pine-scented air fresheners from the trees between the Church and the pig farm. This had only given the smell of pig shit a nauseatingly sweet synthetic overlay that was worse than the smell of shit itself. One desperate summer, Father Ignatius had rented, at great expense, several large fans to blow the odor away. This required a generator that was so loud no one could hear Mass.

The biggest obstacle was that Johnny Pacheco was not a Catholic and had no sympathy for the parishioners or pilgrims who came to the Church. Johnny was not a Protestant either. If anything, he was an agnostic (although he was not familiar with that term) who didn't give a damn about the Church. To him, the smell of pigs was the smell of money, and that was a sweet aroma in his nostrils.

One warm Sunday morning, when the odor was especially noxious, Father Ignatius put away his prepared homily, and went on a rant against Johnny Pacheco and his pigs. Father Ignatius's English was not good in the best of circumstances, and when he was angry he abandoned English altogether and railed away in Spanish.

"Doggone it!" he said several times, but then he'd go back to Spanish. He said that the stink was a sacrilege and an affront to Mary in particular. He said that Johnny Pacheco was an agent of the Devil whose soul would burn in hell. He said that enduring the pig smell had been a test of their faith, but that even God was weary of it, and that it was time to act on their faith. He called upon the devout to rise up against Johnny Pacheco and march *en masse* to his farm to demand that he find another place for his pigs or send them all to the slaughterhouse.

The stunned congregation sat as still as statues. Father Ignatius stepped down from his pulpit and strode up the aisle, calling upon his flock to follow him. Reluctantly, the parishioners filed out behind him and walked down the road to Johnny Pacheco's. Most of them knew that Johnny was an unpredictable loner, and that a confrontation could only end badly. Some slipped away, and the others walked along fearfully, several paces behind Father Ignatius.

Johnny heard the priest coming and saw the crowd behind him. He met them at his gate with a shotgun. The pigs looked on, making grunting, snuffling sounds, their snouts shiny and dripping wet.

"Don't come any closer," called Johnny. "You people stay off my property. I don't want to hurt anyone, but I know my rights!"

Father Ignatius continued to rant in Spanish, saying that the pigs were a blasphemy and calling upon God to smite them down with disease and pestilence. Most people in Maravilla, including Johnny, spoke fluent if antiquated Spanish, and such caustic words caused Johnny to fire a barrel of his gun into the air.

"I've had enough of your threats, padre," Johnny yelled. "You call off your God-fearin' followers and leave me alone, or you better start praying, 'cause I won't waste the other barrel shootin' it into the air."

"I am a man of peace, doggone it!" shouted Father Ignatius belligerently. He struggled for the English words he wanted, but soon gave up. "You are a cowardly heathen pig farmer," he sputtered in Spanish. "I dare you to shoot me! God will protect me!" At that moment the wrath of God entered Father Ignatius, along with a heavy dose of human rage, and he charged at Johnny Pacheco, who was so surprised that he did nothing. Father Ignatius clambered over the gate, grabbed the barrel of the gun and thrust it skyward just as Johnny pulled the trigger. The buckshot blew the leaves off an apple tree in Johnny's front yard and fell harmlessly back to earth. Johnny flung the shotgun away and began to grapple with the priest while his faithful flock looked on in horror and excitement.

Johnny Pacheco was a short, burly man, dressed in his farmer's overalls, while Father Ignatius was a slight man in glasses dressed in his elaborate Sunday robes of white and gold. Johnny seized him by the frock and backed him up to the fence enclosing the pigs. He pushed the gate open and shoved the priest into the pig yard. But Father Ignatius had managed to wrap one hand around the straps of Johnny's overalls and pulled him in the yard too. They both landed in six inches of mud and pig poop, and rolled around on the ground together. Pacheco's pigs were used to Johnny, but they sniffed curiously at Father Ignatius and sampled his robes. The priest stuck his hand in the muck and smeared it all over Johnny's face, while Johnny tried to push the padre into even deeper piles of slop. Before long, seeing the open gate, the pigs began to trot out of their yard to explore the forbidden world outside their pen.

The congregation climbed up onto Johnny's fleet of broken-down cars and trucks that had rusted into place, both to watch the brawl and to get out of the way of Johnny's pigs, which were rumored to be meaner than feral dogs. By now both men were covered in a brown ooze: the thick hair on Johnny's arms and beard was matted with muck, and Father Ignatius's cassock had never been farther from its usual pristine state.

Eventually, someone had called the police and a sheriff's car came careening into the yard, siren wailing. It being a Sunday, there was only one deputy in the car, who quickly assessed the situation and decided there was nothing he could do, short of stepping into the middle of the fight at the risk of getting covered with pig shit. That, he decided, was not an option. So all he could do was to stand by the gate and yell at the fighters. "Cut it out, you guys! You're acting like children! Johnny, all your pigs have escaped. You better get after them." And so on. But his words fell on deaf ears and the two combatants continued to brawl until they were both exhausted and lay in the filth, unable to launch another attack.

Finally, Father Ignatius pushed himself up and wiped off his face with a more or less clean undergarment, spitting out pig shit like tobacco juice. Johnny Pacheco struggled to his feet and hung over the fence, trying to catch his breath. "Hell of a fight, padre. Hell of a fight," he said. He turned and held out his hand to pull the priest out of the muck.

Catching Johnny's pigs proved to be an almost impossible task. They had scattered in all directions. Despite their bulk and short legs, pigs are wily and difficult to capture, made even harder because they weigh up to 200 pounds. So Father Ignatius and a few others, trying to curry favor with their difficult neighbor, spent the afternoon rounding up pigs, using nets and lassos and bribes of carrots. It was nearly dark when they finally corralled the last pig. Johnny was encrusted with pig dung, head to toe. He walked down to the river, stripped off his clothes, and plunged into the chilly water, scrubbing his head and arms until most of the filth was washed away. Father Ignatius staggered back to the rectory looking like the Grim Reaper himself.

From that day on, Johnny Pacheco had a quiet respect for Father Ignatius. He became a regular at mass, and he adopted one of the flower beds in the courtyard of the church. As for his part, Father Ignatius decided that tolerance was an underrated virtue, and adopted the position that seemingly bad things, such as the smell of pig poop, were all part of God's plan, just as much as the Holy Air.

Chapter IV, in which Tai-Keiko notices an itch

The freighter was slow. It chugged along at .63 light years per second. At this rate Tai-Keiko would be an old woman by the time she reached Zeton-9. She had to find a spaceport where she could refuel her banged-up spacebug, repair the resonance coil and the gravity generator. Finally, she detected a deep space garage to which she could transport in 5-4-3-2-1 . . . .

A few weeks earlier Tai-Keiko had noticed that the quantum-chip implanted in her wrist was beginning to itch. She had survived the close encounters that came her way, but they had slowed her mission down, and now her wrist was itching. She would like to reach Zeton-9 and relinquish the Formula. The job would be done and her body would be intact. The human body was not designed to house a quantum-chip for more than a month. After that, the anti-matter plasma layer could be in dan-

ger of leaking, which would mean certain death for the wearer of the chip and loss of the data. There were other copies of the Formula, but this one would disintegrate and never reach Zeton-9. Neither would Tai-Keiko.

The ultimate danger was a chain reaction. Anti-matter plasma, when uncontained, can spread quickly and cause leakage in other pools of a-m plasma. When a critical mass is reached, a leak may jump to another quadrant entirely, taking on a life of its own, until, theoretically, the entire universe is contaminated with the toxic gas released by the anti-matter plasma. This is a worst-case scenario. Sometimes the a-m plasma remains inert and there is no contamination or toxic gas, but that is an unpredictable phenomenon, a random happening, an unexpected twist. And Tai-Keiko did not want to pin her hopes on luck alone. She wanted to get that chip out of her body and into a safe place.

With these thoughts in mind, Tai-Keiko arrived at the space garage, a funky grease-pit in an out-of-the-way slot in the space-time continuum. At this garage, there were four droids working on space vehicles. Tai-Keiko dialed in "English" in the language field and spoke to one of them. She explained what she needed to have done. The grease monkey scratched his neck with his blackened fingers and pushed back his hat.

"Yeah, we can fix 'er. Can't get to it 'til tomorrah though."

"Tomorrow?" exclaimed Tai-Keiko. "There is no tomorrow in space, so you mean, like, never."

"We are pretty backed up, cap."

"Look, how about you just lend me your tools. All right?"

"Sure," said the droid. "Knock yourself out."

"Might need a few parts from you."

"No problem, cap."

Tai-Keiko patched her spacebug together and filled the fuel coils. This would cost her 2.19 days of her life when the Final Reckoning came, but it was worth it to get to Zeton-9. The quantum-chip was bothering her more now. Her skin right around the chip was raw and red. The chip was beginning to push out through the skin.

She tried some maneuvers on the spacebug, just to make sure everything was working, set a course for Zeton-9, and off she went.

To Be Continued...

Chapter Ten

Paloma Medina and Sylvia da Silva were best friends. The two girls lived near each other and were the same age. They were in the same class at school. They liked the same movies and music. As youngsters, they both wore ponytails. People in Maravilla called them the "Bobbsey Twins," even though most people had no idea where the name came from.

Beyond that, "The Twins" were as different as A and zed, zig and zag, zero and a zillion. Sylvia was shy and spoke in a whisper. She avoided the limelight and yet was sought out by her friends, in private, when they were feeling down or confused, when they were blue, because Sylvia was soothing and understanding. She didn't always have a solution, but she made people feel better anyway. In contrast, Paloma was a joker, always ready with a quip or a quote, often in the form of a *dicho* she had heard Pilar say all her life.

"*De noche todos los gatos son pardos*," she would say, apropos of nothing. "At night all cats are gray, right? I love that. It's like, underneath everyone's the same, like the emperor without his clothes."

At home The Twins both faced a tough time. Paloma's father was killed in a car accident when she was three; a few years later she couldn't remember him at all. She was raised by her mother, Pilar, who was a fierce and domineering presence. Pilar was strict with Paloma but loving. She was a big-boned, overweight woman with a booming voice that commanded compliance, saved from being overbearing by her belly laugh which bubbled up every now and then like lava in a volcano. Paloma, in contrast, had a ready grin, a slender figure, and an ability to fill in the dead spaces with a joke. Or she would say, "Doesn't that remind you of a *dicho*, Mom?" This allowed her to float through childhood in good cheer, despite her demanding mother. For the past few years, Paloma watched her mother learn to walk with two canes, although Pilar spent much of her time in a wheelchair since she was overweight and her hips were worn out. This did not stop Pilar from running her house and store with an iron fist.

Also in the house was Paloma's paternal grandfather (Pilar's father-in-law), Oscar, who came to live with them when he lost his son in the car accident, which also took his wife. Oscar helped out at the store and kept the books. Pilar badgered him mercilessly, telling him what needed to be done and how to do it. She kept her receipts in one box and her bills in another, and expected Oscar to sort it all out. Oscar said it would be much easier to track everything on a computer, but Pilar had an irrational suspicion of electronic recordkeeping. To the frustration of Oscar, she had a mind that remembered every detail of her business. Her inventory of over 500 different items was stored in her brain. Dealing with dozens of vendors, she knew their pricing, even though the prices fluctuated from one order to the next. She pretended not to understand why Oscar couldn't do the same, and claimed that using a computer was the sign of a weak mind.

The other "twin," Sylvia, lived with her parents, Alice and Luis, in a trailer home they rented from Pilar. Alice hated that trailer. She was always bumping into a misplaced chair or stepping on the cat's tail. She blamed her perpetual sinus problems on the carpet or the insulation. To make things worse (both her allergies and other matters in her life), Alice worked from home, doing customer service surveys over the phone. She was stuck in the house all day while people hung up on her; some even cursed her.

Sylvia was the only light shining in Alice's dim world. Like Paloma, Sylvia attended the community college, taking courses in bookkeeping and accounting. Without being asked, Sylvia helped with household chores and was usually able to keep the peace between her polarized parents, timid Alice and the volatile Luis.

Alice was afraid of Luis. Ever since he returned from combat in Iraq, Luis was a man with two personalities. Although Alice was a kind and gentle soul, she aroused Luis's passions—be they love or anger, gratitude or disgust. Sometimes he worshipped Alice, showering her with unexpected gifts, taking her out dancing or to a movie, and fixing up the house as needed. But when he drank—when he drank heavily—he became a monster. He would fly into a rage over a small thing, like dirty socks or an unmade bed. He would break dishes or vases, throw chairs. Insults flew from his mouth like yellowjackets. He cursed like a convict and, worst of all, he would beat Alice.

A lot of things in life are funny, but getting beaten up isn't one of them. The Hollywood image of a victim joking his way through a beating (a fist slams into the poor bastard's stomach, ha-ha), just to aggravate his attackers (a knee hits his groin, hee-hee-hee), is as fake as false teeth. The poor sucker grins diabolically (knuckles crack a jaw, haw-haw); he's tough enough to take it . . . . That's a lie. Only twisted, tortured souls would wisecrack their way through an assault. More than once as a child, Luis saw his father getting beaten, because he ran with bad people who did bad things, but never once did he see his father laughing or mocking his tormentors. No, if he could speak at all, he would be pleading for them to stop, making promises he couldn't possibly keep, anything to stop the pain of the pounding. Luis would try to intervene, yelling at them to leave his dad alone, bravely grabbing the arm of one of the thugs, who would fling off Luis like a bug saying, "You stay out of this, kid. Stay out of it and keep your mouth shut, or we'll give your old man even worse." In Luis's father, the pain and humiliation of being beaten turned into anger, anger that he released by beating Luis, so the boy was punched around by the very man he sought to defend. Oh, these were not funny memories, not funny at all. But even though Luis knew what a terrifying thing it was to be beaten by two or three guys, he never learned any other way to settle a dispute. He always tried to run, first of all, but he couldn't always get away. He learned that in his life, so far, fighting was the ultimate decision-maker, power the supreme enforcer. Fighting in Iraq only reinforced this belief. So Luis had two faces, and brutality was central to one of them.

It was true that Luis had been abused as a child. It was also true that he had not received the promotion he had recently applied for at work, which would have meant better pay and benefits. But these things did not change or justify the events that took place the following Friday night. No joke.

Luis had gone out to Red's Blue Chile Tavern, leaving Alice at home with Sylvia and Paloma. The Twins were in Sylvia's room, talking and designing fanciful dresses. Alice was in the living room watching TV.

At the bar, New Mexican polkas were blaring out of the jukebox, tequila and beer were flowing as fast as Red could pour them, and the air was thick with cigarette smoke, even though smoking was prohibited by law. The room was filled with laughter and loud voices speaking Spanish peppered with English. Jake was one of the few white faces there, and there were even fewer women—of any shade.

The pool table was in heavy use, and some men were betting on games or even on specific shots. Jake played a game of stripes and solids, but lost by one ball. Luis had been drinking beer laced with shots of tequila when he declared he wanted to play a few games of pool. He played poorly, and the more he drank, the worse he played.

"Give it up, Luis," someone said. "You're getting your ass kicked."

"One more game," said Luis. "I can feel it now. I'm gonna run the table." Derisive laughter rebutted his claim. Nobody wanted to play him, and this made Luis angry. "Come on, *pachucos*. Don't none of you shitheads have the guts to play me?" No one answered, and the bar quieted down, as patrons stopped talking to watch the drama.

"I think you've had enough, Luis," said Red. "You better go on home."

"Hell, no! I ain't going nowhere until someone gives me a game. One more game." Luis looked around the room. "How 'bout you, whitey," he said to Jake.

"I don't think so, man," replied Jake. "I'm not good enough to beat you." Luis took this as sarcasm, and he didn't like it.

"What are you, chicken?"

"That's right, I'm chicken." Jake made a sound like a chicken, trying to defuse the situation with self-deprecating humor. Some people laughed, but Luis felt insulted.

"What are you even doing here, chickenshit?" Luis demanded. "Why'n't you go back to wherever you came from?" He could tell this stung Jake. "Where *are* you from, white boy?"

"Sigma III, in the Andromeda galaxy. Ever been there?"

"You wise-ass son of a bitch." He raised the pool cue to take a swing at Jake, and three guys jumped on him to prevent it.

"I think you better go, Jake," said Red. "This is only gonna get worse for you."

"Right," said Jake. "See you later."

"I'll get you someday, you honky fucker!" yelled Luis. The three men held him back as Jake walked out of the bar and drove away.

"Time to go home, Luis," Red said. "Go sleep it off." Someone offered to give Luis a ride home.

"I don't need no fuckin' ride! Think I'm a cripple? I can drive my own fuckin' self." He left, slamming the door behind him. Everyone in the tavern heard his engine roar to life and heard him peel out, spewing gravel behind him.

Red called Alice on the phone. "Alice," he said, "Luis is on his way home and he's really drunk and angry. I thought you should know."

Alice didn't know what to do. She locked the doors and thought maybe she should take the girls over to Pilar's house. But before she could act on that impulse, Luis came squealing into the yard. Alice heard the car door slam and heard Luis's footsteps come up the steps. He tried to open the door. "What the fuck?" he said to nobody. "Alice!" he yelled. "Alice, you in there? Open the fuckin' door."

Alice plucked up her courage. "Go away, Luis," she said. "Go away or I'll call the cops."

"The fuck you will." Luis broke the door's glass with his fist, reached inside and unlocked the deadbolt. "Think you can lock me out of my own house?" he demanded. "Think again, bitch."

"Luis, I'm sorry. It's just that . . ." Luis stepped through the door and hit her across the face with the back of his hand. Alice fell to the floor, blood trickling from her lip.

Sylvia and Paloma heard the fight and ran to find out what was happening. "Get back in your room, Sylvia," yelled Luis when he saw them. "Both of you!" They did, but not before they saw Alice lying on the floor, a purple welt darkening on her cheek. Back in Sylvia's room, Paloma immediately called 9-1-1. From downstairs came the sound of flesh hitting flesh and bone hitting bone, along with Alice's cries and whimpers.

"My friend's father is beating up her mother," Paloma said to the 9-1-1 operator. She gave them the address. "Please hurry. He's really drunk." Then she called home and told Pilar what was happening.

"I'll be right there," said Pilar. Leaning on her canes, Pilar hoisted herself to her feet and made her way out the door.

Alice curled herself into a fetal position.

"Please, Luis. Don't hurt me. What did I do wrong?"

"You married me, you stupid *puta*," said Luis. "I'm scum and you're a scum-sucking sow." He kicked her savagely in the ribs, and Alice cried out in pain.

The Twins huddled together in a corner of Sylvia's bedroom. The family cat ran across the room and hid under the bed. In a gesture of great bravery, timid Sylvia ventured out, followed by Paloma. "Stop it, Daddy!" she yelled. "Leave her alone."

"Oh, you want some of this too? You always take her side." Luis picked up a table lamp and threw it down the hallway at Sylvia, but it missed her and crashed into the back wall.

Pilar clumped up the steps. "Luis? Alice?" she growled. "What's going on?" The front door was open and glass littered the floor. She heard the lamp smash into the wall. Luis grabbed Alice by her arms, squeezed hard and shook her, then threw her against the sofa. "You married a loser, Alice, which makes you a dumb bitch." Luis was about to hit Alice again when Pilar whacked him across his back with her cane. This enraged Luis, who turned on Pilar.

"Stay out of this, you old cripple!" he yelled, pushing her to the ground. At that moment, red and blue flashing lights appeared in the driveway. A state trooper stepped out of his car, holding a Taser. He advanced on the house, pointing the Taser at Luis.

"Everyone freeze!" he said in a commanding voice. "You!" he said, waggling his Taser at Luis, "lie face down on the floor." Instead, Luis, still filled with the adrenaline of anger and frustration, ran out the door and leaped over the steps towards the policeman. The Taser's shock hit Luis at the top of his jump, and he landed on the ground like a rag doll. The cop handcuffed his hands behind his back. Then he called for an ambulance.

When the EMTs came, they examined Alice first. Her body was badly bruised. X-rays at the hospital revealed she had two broken ribs. They taped her up, gave her two pain pills and sent her home with Sylvia and Paloma. Luis spent the night in a holding tank with three other petty criminals. His whole body ached from the electric jolt. Alice wouldn't bail him out, and Luis didn't have enough dough of his own.

That night, Alice and Sylvia stayed at Pilar's. Alice stayed in Pilar's bed, the girls slept in Paloma's bed, and Pilar took the couch. No one slept very well. At some late hour, Sylvia turned to Paloma and cried uncontrollably.

Overnight the pain pills wore off. Alice was still feeling pain strong enough to make her sick to her stomach. She had a prescription for more pills, but OxyContin was expensive and Alice had little money and no insurance. She already owed money to Pilar. Out of desperation—partly for the pain but mostly for the mental relief the pills delivered—she called her uncle Jimmy, a plumber who dealt drugs on the side.

Alice asked Uncle Jimmy if he had any pain pills. Jimmy said, sure, but they weren't free. Alice said okay, but could she get some on credit? Jimmy said, maybe. How long 'til she could pay up? Alice said, maybe a month. Jimmy said, okay, I'll give you three weeks' worth, and your first payment is due in two weeks. Alice agreed. Jimmy came over with the pills within half an hour.

Later that same morning, at the arraignment, an attorney showed up from the public defenders' office to represent four accused men, including Luis. He spoke to each of them. When it was Luis's turn, his attorney told him not to say anything. "Let me do the talking," he said. "The only things you have to say are your full name and address at the beginning and then "Guilty" or "Not Guilty" at the end. Now, you are charged with assault on a family member. Tell me what happened."

Luis sat in silence for a moment, not wanting to face facts. "I had a lousy day," he said finally. "I didn't get this promotion at work. But I should have. I earned that fucker."

"So you were angry about not getting the promotion," said the p.d.

"Yeah."

"What'd you do?"

"I got drunk at the Blue Chile. I was having an argument with this guy, and I was going to whack him with a pool cue, but some other guys jumped me. So I left. And when I got home, the door was locked. I yell at Alice to open it up, but she says no. So I bust through the window and open the door from the inside. Then I . . . I don't know, it's hard to remember. I guess I must have wailed on Alice, but all I remember is rage, and then the damn Taser exploded, and I was down for the count."

"Sounds like 'guilty' to me," said the p.d. "It's your first offense, so practice looking real sorry, because a lenient judge is the only hope you've got."

Luis could have been tried on a felony rap, but Alice and Sylvia refused to testify against him. He got six months of community service, which was mostly delivering wood and groceries to old people. He also had to attend meetings at the rehab center.

With Pilar's encouragement, Alice filed for divorce. Luis refused to move out. While the divorce was pending, they lived in the unbearable presence of one another, making an effort to be civil, although anger bubbled slowly under the surface. Even now they had an undeniable attraction to one another that had expressed itself in a range of ways, from lust and wild sexual tussles to gloves-off shouting matches to actually throwing punches. The court granted the divorce and mandated that Luis move out and stay away from Alice. Alice was awarded some alimony, but not enough to live on. Luis rarely paid it anyway.

During this time, Alice continued to take pain pills. After her body was healed, she still felt wounded in her psyche. Alice had never been a strong person, and in any conflict she became the victim. This was a role that wore her to exhaustion. The pain pills helped. She had started with the pink 20s which Uncle Jimmy sold her for $10 each. They were time-release pills, and one would keep her free of pain all day. Before long, though, one-a-day was not enough, and Jimmy moved her up to yellow 40s for $20 each. Then Alice discovered that if she chewed them, the pills would release all their power at once, giving her a euphoric high. By the time her body was healed, Alice was hooked, and she took the pills just to feel good. The drug made her happy and energetic, but by the end of the day, she would begin to feel shaky and then desperate. She set up a regular schedule to get the pills from Jimmy.

The yellow 40s had jumped to $25 each, and paying for them was difficult for Alice. She had no savings, except for a jar of change on her dresser, containing more nickels than quarters. Alice had relied on Luis to pay the bills, and once he was gone, so was the money for food and gas and everything else. Pilar offered her a job at the store. It was almost time for Paloma to go back to school, her second year at the community college, and Alice could take over her job. Pilar knew Alice was taking pills for her depression, but she didn't realize the depth of her dependence or the devilishly strong grip of opioids. Sylvia was aware—because of the regular visits from Uncle Jimmy—and Sylvia had seen what happened to her mother when she didn't have any more pills: anxiety, vomiting, achiness, like the worst case of the flu ever. And rather than see her mother suffer, she became complicit in Alice's addiction, doling out her pills to her in a regulated way. Uncle Jimmy suggested she try heroin, which was much cheaper, but Alice had a lifelong fear of needles.

When Paloma's classes began, Alice took over her job at Maravilla Blessings. She barely made enough money to pay for groceries and utilities and rent, and so, to pay for her habit she began stealing thirty or forty dollars a week from the cash register. Oscar knew what was happening, but, without a word to anyone, he protected Alice by making false entries in the books to cover the losses.

Chapter Eleven

Uncle Jimmy had met his usual connection at the usual time in the usual parking lot. As usual, he stashed the drugs in the trunk of his car underneath a blanket. After that, his day took an unusual turn.

Jimmy's Rule #1 was to go straight home after a drug buy and move the drugs to the floor safe in his bedroom. But that day he said to hell with the rules, and he decided to stop off at Red's Blue Chile Tavern for a beer and a couple of minis. Two guys he knew from high school were drinking shots of tequila and light beer; they invited Jimmy to join them. Before long they were reminiscing about the old days when they were in high school, and how much fun they had. Actually, they hated high school, and ditched classes whenever they could, and that's when the fun began.

During the day they would just hang out by the river and smoke cigarettes and drink Cokes. Sometimes one of them would have a BB gun, then they would drop an empty Coke can off the bridge upstream, and they'd take turns trying to nail the can as it floated down the river. This was harmless fun, but enjoyed at the expense of their education. Nighttime was best because they could do things under the cover of darkness that they couldn't do during the day.

Tagging was a major pursuit. At first they bought the cans of spray paint over the counter, but the cops quickly figured out—by grilling the cashier—who had bought a lot of spray paint lately. Jimmy and the boys were hauled in for questioning, threatened by the cops to stop their vandalizing, admonished to start attending school, quit screwing around. Of course the boys all agreed to this in order to get out of there. They were released to the custody of their parents, which was hardly any better than the cops. After that, it became part of their tagging protocol that a true tag artist would steal his paint.

With great hilarity, they remembered the time they were tagging the post office when a state trooper drove by and saw the activity. Jimmy and the boys took off running up the arroyo toward their car they had left on a side road. They could hear the cop hustling after them, his flashlight beam waving spasmodically as he ran. The young vandals reached their car and sped away in a cloud of dust, leaving the state cop gasping for breath a half mile from his patrol car. Out of spite, they swung back around to the post office and tagged the patrol car while the trooper was still trudging back down the arroyo.

Then there was the time they took Rudy Abeyta's hot rod out to a flat and deserted road to see if Rudy could get it up to 120 miles per hour and how long it would take to go two miles. The car was a beautifully restored 1958 Chevy Impala, with a tasteful two-tone paint job, and a little extra under the hood to help with acceleration. For the time trial, they had stolen a set of walkie-talkies and two stopwatches from the school's athletics office. They measured off the distance, spraying a white stripe every quarter mile for two miles. Rudy, being very safety-minded, had installed a seat belt because seat belts weren't standard equipment in 1958. He put on a helmet he had acquired in trade for a grill from a '55 Chevy pickup. The truck had been abandoned on the side of the road for more than 24 hours. After that Rudy and his friends felt it was fair game, so they stripped it clean, and Rudy got the grill.

Rudy climbed into his car and revved the engine a few times. The two guys on the walkie-talkies synchronized their stopwatches and then counted down to take off. "Five, four, three, two, one, Go!" was the command. Rudy pressed the accelerator down, quickly but smoothly, got some RPMs, speed-shifted from first to third. The speedometer read 60 MPH. Rudy stayed in third until he hit 70, then went to fourth and cruised up to 100 MPH. The white markers went by at increasingly shorter intervals. Rudy pressed the accelerator to the floor and let the motor catch up: 110, 115, 120! When he crossed the two-mile marker, he was doing 135.

Rudy slowed down and carefully turned around toward his *chucos*. The speedometer read 60, but it felt like 25 to Rudy. Then a coyote jumped out of the brush beside the road and streaked across the road. Rudy stepped on the brakes and swerved a bit, but hit the coyote anyway. The coyote flipped off the front of the car and smacked into the windshield, blocking Rudy's view. Rudy slammed the breaks and braced for an impact with something. He ran off the road into the sagebrush and rolled to a stop. Rudy was unhurt, the car was bloodied but otherwise undamaged, and the coyote was dead. In a few minutes they were all yipping like coyotes.

Uncle Jimmy and the boys laughed as they recalled these youthful adventures, and had another shot of tequila. By the time Jimmy was ready to go home, he was plastered. But being plastered doesn't always stop people from driving, and it didn't stop Jimmy. *I don't even live a mile away*, he reminded himself.

A pack of motorcycle riders on a 100-mile ride was coming from the other direction. It was late afternoon and the sun was in their eyes. Jimmy was swerving down the road, trying to stay on his side of the center stripe but not always succeeding. He saw the bikers coming, but something on the road, perhaps a dead cat, made him swerve toward the middle, and he hit the first biker head on. The next couple of bikers glanced off Jimmy's car and went out of control. When the dust settled, the first biker lay dead in the road. The others had escaped with scrapes, bruises and a few broken bones.

Jimmy was unhurt and a little confused about what had happened. His car had run into a tree and a fountain of water spurted from the radiator.

Jimmy sat in the road by his car, trying to figure it out. He was still sitting there when the cops arrived a few minutes later. They booked Jimmy for vehicular homicide, DWI, and reckless driving, and locked him in the county jail. They impounded his car. Later, when the police were examining the car, they found the drugs in the trunk. That added a few more criminal counts to his charges.

Alice had been waiting anxiously for Jimmy. He was never late (Rule #2: Be on time), but now it was two hours past their usual time. She left a message on his cell phone, which rang from within a plastic bag that held his personal possessions in a police storage locker. Jimmy had admonished Alice *never* to go to his house. (Rule #3: Don't allow customers to come to your house.) He would always come to her. But today he didn't show. Alice had enough OxyContin to last through the next two days— she always kept an emergency stash—but it made her nervous when she had to borrow from it. To calm herself down and counter her anxiety, she took another pill that evening.

Over the months Alice had become more and more dependent on the oxy. She was up to 60s now. She carefully opened the capsule, put the powder in a line, and snorted it up her nose through a cut straw. The effect was immediate and powerful. She felt blissful, powerful and free from worry.

Money was an issue. Alice had used up her reserves and had finally gone to a Fast Check for a short-term, high-interest loan. Uncle Jimmy suggested she go on heroin. He said it was much cheaper and less edgy-feeling. Alice wanted to quit. She wanted to get clean. But she was reluctant to go to Narcotics Anonymous. She was afraid to admit she had lost complete control of herself and needed help.

Alice was awake most of the night. She went through alternate spells of chills and fevers; she tried taking a hot bath, which felt good even though she was sneezing incessantly. Both nausea and the runs assaulted her. Moving from the bath and the bed to the toilet was painful in itself; every muscle ached. She longed for sleep, but it was dawn before she got any. That morning, Alice was due at the store at 9:00, and Sylvia woke her up at 8:00. Alice looked haggard and felt sick.

"What's the matter, Mom?" asked Sylvia. "You look terrible."

"Uncle Jimmy didn't show yesterday. I'm down to my last pill."

"Oh, God. Well, swallow it whole; don't snort it, so you can get through the day. I'll try to track down Jimmy."

"Thanks, honey." Alice took her last pill and began to feel better immediately. But by the end of the day she was sweating and her muscles were beginning to ache again.

"What's wrong, Alice?" asked Pilar. "You look sick."

"I think I'm coming down with the flu," said Alice.

"You better go home to bed. Tell Sylvia to make you some chicken soup."

Sylvia didn't have to look hard to find Jimmy. The story in the newspaper said he was being held in the county jail without bail on charges of DWI and vehicular homicide, and drug possession.

The next few days were pure hell for Alice. She had no other drug connection, so she suffered the terrible miseries of withdrawal. Sylvia tried to help by scoring some oxy for her mom. She drove into town that evening. Everyone hanging out on a corner or cruising in a low-rider looked like a drug dealer to her, but she didn't know how to approach them. And she was afraid—afraid of getting caught buying drugs, afraid of making a mistake, afraid of getting ripped off or assaulted. She drove back home empty-handed, crying all the way.

At home she found her mother curled up in a fetal position, shivering uncontrollably. "I'm cold," she said to Sylvia, who covered her with blankets, gave her aspirin and made some soup for her. Alice was moaning and making inarticulate animal sounds. She vomited until her stomach was empty; then she had the dry heaves. Sylvia was thoroughly frightened and thought of taking her mother to the hospital, but they didn't have insurance, and most of all, she didn't want Pilar to find out that Alice was an addict. Afraid that Alice might try to kill herself, Sylvia stayed up all night with her, holding her, and singing in a soothing tone until they both fell asleep as the birds began to sing.

At 10:00 Pilar called to ask about Alice; she hadn't opened the store at 9:00. Sylvia explained that her mother had a bad case of the flu and that they had both been up all night. Pilar said to take the day off and call her in the evening. Alice was delirious most of the day and hallucinating that weasels were running over her and biting her, tearing off bits of flesh from her face and ears. By nightfall the drug dragon had retreated briefly, releasing Alice from its claws and fangs. She fell into a deep sleep, but awoke in the night drenched in sweat, burning up yet shivering in her damp clothes. The next day was more of the same. Mid-afternoon her fever finally broke, and the worst was over. Alice took the rest of the week off to recover. Sylvia was exhausted and hungry, but their pantry was empty, so she went to the grocery store to stock up. When she got home, she poured two glasses of orange juice and gave one to Alice. To Alice, orange juice had never tasted so good.

Chapter V, in which Tai-Keiko flees the Krossarian wardogs

Tai-Keiko landed in a deep gorge with rocky outcroppings above her. A few scrubby plants grew out of the rocks. She adjusted her shield to blend in with the unfamiliar terrain. She had the sense that she was being watched, that a thousand eyes were tracking her every move. The natives knew how to hide in this landscape. But here Tai-Keiko was the alien. She wondered if the natives were friendly, hostile or merely curious.

Nothing stirred. Even the air was still. Her chrontonometer placed her near the north pole of a small planet named Dromodius. At the equator it was cold and icy, but the poles were hot and dry.

She had been forced to land by a pair of Krossarian fighters who were undoubtedly looking for her now. Landing had been the easy part. Escaping would be harder. Somewhere out there the Krossarian warriors were waiting and watching for her. Already they would be dredging the planet floor with their invisible microtron nets.

In a tree covered with thick blue leaves, something moved, something red and small. It fluttered and then disappeared. Red was the imperial color of the Krossarians, but surely they wouldn't show their colors here. Unless . . . unless it was a decoy. Tai-Keiko wouldn't take the bait, if that's what it was. Instead, she moved her spacebug soundlessly along the planet floor, moving slowly, all systems alert to any movement.

She looked up at the sky, green as a lily pad, a few yellow clouds floating by. Ten meters in front of her she saw another flash of red, and this time she knew what it was: a spy drone. By now it would have flashed Tai-Keiko's coordinates to the Krossarian warriors, and they would soon be upon her. There was no point in hiding any more. Tai-Keiko ignited the engines and began her ascent. A Krossarian wardog was on her heels, climbing the cliff, trying to get out of the gorge before Tai-Keiko did. She and the wardog reached the plateau at the same time. The wardog leaped for the spaceship, landing on top of it. Tai-Keiko engaged in a series of jarring maneuvers, trying to knock the wardog off the ship. The wardog finally lost its grip and slid off the spacebug but, at the last second, gained a grasp on the landing gear. Tai-Keiko banked abruptly towards the cliff and slammed the wardog into a sharp rock. The dog yowled and fell away. Tai-Keiko accelerated up and out of the gorge, and from there into space, free, at least momentarily, from the Krossarians.

To Be Continued...

Chapter Twelve

Judge Evan George was having the time of his life. It had been determined that the hearing could not take place in either county, for that would be prejudicial. So they moved the hearing to an outlying county, and it fell to Judge George to hear the case.

Judge George was delighted to have a case more interesting than traffic citations or drunk and disorderlies. And the media would be there, too. He knew that the defendants' lawyers would be smart and well-prepared, so he studied the Constitution, the statutes and precedents. He would act completely without bias, he would keep the hearing on track, he would control the courtroom. Judge George would rule on all motions, and his word would be law. This was going to be fun.

The only lawyer in Maravilla was Pete Gonzales. He had not practiced in years—and when he had, it was water law, not Constitutional law—but it didn't seem smart to bring in an outsider. This was all about local control. Pete was well-known and respected, plus he was a likeable person and a good speaker. He wasn't imperious like Pilar. Pete had been slow to support the revolt, but he saw the community coming together, and he got swept up in the movement. He was flattered to be offered the job, but nervous as he sat at the plaintiff's table with Pilar and Sylvia.

At the defendants' table were four lawyers of various ages in sharp-looking suits. The two county attorneys had each hired an extra attorney to help them prepare their case. They had thick binders of information, a container full of sharp pencils, and legal pads to scribble on.

"All rise," said the bailiff. Everyone stood as Judge George came in through a side door. Tall, thin and balding, draped in black, Judge George surveyed the courtroom over the top of his spectacles perched on the lower half of his nose. He tried to look grave, but inside he was giggling with glee. He took his seat and so did everyone else.

The court had not allowed the community of Maravilla to be the plaintiff, since it was neither an incorporated entity nor an individual. So Pilar had agreed to stand in for Maravilla.

The bailiff called out, "Pilar Medina vs. Rio Grande County and Carson County."

The strategy of the Maravillosos was simple: rely on a strict interpretation of the Constitution, which does not refer to "people" and does not rule out pets. The strategy of the two counties was also simple: argue that Maravilla did not meet the Constitutional requirement in New Mexico for a county to have a population of 10,000 or more.

After an hour of legal maneuvering by the two counties—trying to get the case dismissed for a variety of reasons—Judge George banged his gavel. "Enough of this legal posturing and citing of irrelevant precedents," he said. The Judge looked right at Pete Gonzales and said, "The Court will entertain your argument, sir, as to why the community of Maravilla should be allowed to form its own county."

"Thank you, Your Honor. I would refer the Court to the Constitution of the state of New Mexico, Article X, section 5, which outlines the requirements and the procedures for incorporating a county. It says that if the area of the county 'is less than one hundred forty-four square miles in area and has a population of ten thousand or more,' it 'may become an incorporated county by the following procedure.' The procedure says we must file a petition containing the signatures of at least ten percent of the registered voters in the proposed county, and that then the Governor will appoint a charter commission to draft a county charter. This proposed charter, it says, shall be submitted to the voters of the county—in this case two counties—within one year, and 'if adopted by a majority of the qualified voters voting in the election, the county shall become an incorporated county.'

"Now, Your Honor, this seems pretty clear to me. First, the area we are talking about is only about 25 square miles, so we meet that condition. Second, we can document that our population is over ten thousand. Third, we have submitted a petition to the Commissions of Rio Grande and Carson Counties containing the signatures of well over ten percent of the registered voters in Maravilla. So, having met the constitutional requirements, I would ask the Court to direct the Governor to appoint a charter commission to draft a charter for Maravilla County. Thank you, Your Honor."

Judge George turned to the attorneys for the two counties and said, "Your response, gentlemen?"

The county attorney for Rio Grande County rose. "Your Honor, we acknowledge the accuracy of Mr. Gonzales's reading of the Constitution, but we take issue with his contention that Maravilla has a population of over ten thousand. According to the last census, the area specified in the petition contains 5,156 people—men, women and children—which is nowhere near the ten thousand required by the Constitution."

"Mr. Gonzales," said the Judge, "how did you determine that the proposed county of Maravilla has over ten thousand people?"

"We don't claim to have over ten thousand people, Your Honor. But the Constitution says nothing about people. It just says 'a population of ten thousand or more.' To reach that amount, we have included our pets and, in fact, any animal with a name. We contend that the Constitution may be interpreted to mean ten thousand *individuals*, not ten thousand people." He paused for dramatic effect during which the counties' attorneys whispered furiously and a buzz went through the courtroom, along with a few titters. Judge George banged his gavel for silence to cover his own dubious surprise. Then Pete picked up a thick sheaf of papers. "I would like to enter this list into the record, as Exhibit A, which contains the names and addresses of over 5000 pets, along with their names and the names of their owners in Maravilla." He handed the bailiff two copies of the list—one for the judge and one for the defendants. The list was filled with names like Crackers, Puffy, Coco and Wiggles, along with their breed, if known, and any distinguishing characteristics ("Loves broccoli!" "Great with children!").

The county attorney for Carson County glanced through the document, then leapt to his feet. "That is the most ludicrous argument I've ever heard, Your Honor. Even if we do concede that the Constitution could mean 'individuals,' is it not patently obvious that pets are not individuals? They can't talk, they can't take care of themselves, they can't work, and they can't vote."

"Mr. Gonzales, how do you respond?" asked the Judge.

Pete Gonzales stood up and said, "Well, your Honor, babies can't talk or take care of themselves. Old people can't work. No one under 18 can vote. Yet we consider all of those people to be individuals."

Judge George turned back to the two counties. "Your Honor," said another of the four buttoned-down attorneys, "if I may expand on my colleague's point. There are numerous things that pets cannot do that individual humans can. For instance, they cannot use tools; they are incapable of reason; they cannot create music or art."

"Your Honor," said Pete Gonzales. "The question is not what people can do versus what pets can do. That argument cuts both ways. Can we run as fast as a racehorse? Can we pounce like a cat? No, the question is: does each pet have its own *individual* talents and abilities? And the answer is 'Yes.' Otherwise, my horse Midnight would run as fast as Secretariat and my cat Betsy would be a good mouser like my other cat, Louie."

There were more chuckles from the crowd. "Quiet!" Judge George said, rapping his gavel.

"Your Honor, I object to this entire ridiculous argument!" exclaimed the attorney for Rio Grande County. "Everyone knows that the authors of the Constitution intended to refer to people, not pets." The Judge looked back to Pete Gonzales.

"Your Honor, no one really knows who the authors were referring to. I'm pretty certain they didn't mean to include Indians or women, since the state Constitution was ratified in 1911 and women didn't get the vote until 1920. Indians in Utah couldn't vote until 1956. I think the counselor from Rio Grande County needs to take a broader view." The county attorney scowled and turned bright red.

Again the onlookers burst into laughter. "Order in the court!" cried the judge.

"Your Honor," said the attorney from Carson County, "I would like to quote from the Constitution of the state of New Mexico, Article II, section 2: 'All political power is vested in and derived from the *people*: all government of right originates with the *people*, is founded upon their will and is instituted solely for their good.' It's clearly about the people. It doesn't say anything about pets."

"Mr. Gonzales?" said the Judge.

"We do not disagree with the defendants, Your Honor. People are in charge, not pets. The government is of the people, by the people and for the people. That means that the people govern all individuals, whether they be people or pets. That's why we have laws against the mistreatment of animals, as well as of people. Look, Your Honor, we're not advocating running a dog for county commissioner, although I've got an Australian Shepherd who would do a better job than some people currently in office." Laughter erupted in the gallery again, and again the judge called for order. "What we're saying is that we all live with our pets, and we know they're all different from each other, they all have their quirks, and that's because they are *individuals*."

"But Your Honor," said one of the county attorneys, "pets don't have souls."

A huge outcry erupted from the Maravillosos crowded into the courtroom. The Judge banged his gavel. "Quiet!" he yelled. "We will have quiet or I'll clear the courtroom." He had always wanted to say that in court.

Gradually the noise subsided, but it was obvious that the good people of Maravilla disagreed with the county attorney.

"Mr. Gonzales," said Judge George, "how do you respond? Do pets have souls?"

"I'm not sure that is a relevant question," Pete said. "But first we would have to answer the question, 'What is a soul?' Pets have personalities. They have likes and dislikes. They recognize one individual from another. They communicate pretty well once you get to know them. They even have emotions. What else do you need to have a soul?"

Judge George paused thoughtfully. "Gentlemen," he said, "It is not our place to say which beings have souls and which do not. That is a matter for God to decide. So I'm going to rule that that question is irrelevant to this hearing. More to the point, Mr. Gonzales has presented sufficient evidence to convince me that pets are indeed individuals. Therefore, since the Constitution does not explicitly exclude pets, Maravilla has a population of more than 10,000 and may form its own county."

A cheer went up in the courtroom. Everyone was clapping and hugging each other and jumping up and down. No one heard Judge George as he banged his gavel and said, "Court adjourned."

Chapter Thirteen

The Cross of Holy Air Catholic Church had been a lovely chapel. Pilgrims who came to worship there were always struck by the perfect symmetry of its design and the deep emotion conveyed by its wooden statuary. The tears on a cheek, the grief in the eyes, the lacerations of the flesh all conveyed a deep despair that only faith could overcome, especially faith in the healing power of the Holy Air. But the works of man, even those of a spiritual nature, are still subject to the ravages of time, and Maravilla's little church was no exception. Over the decades, little had been done to maintain and preserve it, and now it needed attention before it became more of a ruin than a shrine.

Aurelio Salazar V understood this. He also understood the power of good works and the nature of capitalism. He had decided that his son was right: they should repair the church and restore the house. Not because he cared about the church or about Maravilla. He didn't. He based his decision not on the goodness of his heart but on the greediness of his appetites: he thought the investment would make money.

Aurelio V devised a grand plan of three parts. The first part would entail a complete restoration of the church to a condition even more striking and heart-wrenching than its original state. Part two would focus on the old Salazar house. He would demolish what was left of the crumbling building and in its place he would build a replica that would serve as a visitors center and living museum with a gift shop. For a small entrance fee, tourists could tour the house. Guides in period costumes would point out the features of pioneer life in the early nineteenth century and demonstrate the crafts and traditions of the time. The tourists would appreciate a little Jamestown showmanship.

Part three was Aurelio V's favorite. For this he would need to acquire another property in Maravilla. Here he would put the lynchpin for the entire project: a theme park based on Catholic beliefs. Featuring a Ferris wheel and other rides, the carnival would bring in the kids and they would bring their parents. There would be a live nativity scene with the Holy Family; a photographer would be on-hand to snap pictures of the tourists with Mary and Joseph. There would be sheep and goats to pet, burros to ride, and a booth for shooting hoops, offering prizes with a religious theme: cuddly stuffed saints, angel dolls, Bible quotes on coffee mugs, Frisbees featuring an image of the church, and small bottles of Holy Air.

The Holy Air was key. The church was asking for five bucks per vial. Aurelio would give it away free—to anyone who could throw three out of five beanbags through the mouth of St. John the Apostle. The beanbag tosses would cost a dollar each.

Aurelio V kept all of his plans to himself. He asked his son to find a good contractor—one that specialized in older buildings and reconstruction. He wanted a damage assessment of the church building. He didn't want any surprises. He needed to compute a tentative bottom line, at least. A guesstimate. Aurelio V looked at it as an investment: he would make Maravilla into a major tourist destination and reap the rewards. This would be a gold mine.

What the contractor found was not pretty. There were a multitude of minor repairs needed—cracks to patch and leaks to plug—and there were a few major problems too: One of the outdoor walls would have to be restored. Somehow, in spite of the dry climate, water had soaked into the adobe. They would have to strip off the plaster and let the adobe dry out.

"Why bother?" Aurelio V asked the contractor. "We might as well replace the adobe with cement blocks and re-plaster them. No one will know the difference. They'll *look* right."

"Well, maybe you didn't know this," the contractor said, "but this building has been designated by the state as a Historic Cultural Property, and it is on the National Register of Historic Places. You can repair it, but you can't change it."

"What the hell?" Aurelio said. "Says who?"

"The state of New Mexico in a law called the Cultural Properties Protection Act."

"Well, fuck me!" Aurelio exclaimed. "How much would it cost?"

When the contractor gave him his estimate, Aurelio was dumbstruck. "*How* much?" he said. "I don't think I heard you right." But he had.

Aurelio V considered the matter deeply. Before he committed to restoring the church, he wanted to be sure he could build his theme park. He asked a realtor to research properties in the area and found out that the Archdiocese owned most of the vacant land near the church. He devised an offer and arranged an appointment with the Archbishop.

"Your Grace," he said, "as you are aware the church in Maravilla, the Cross of Holy Air, is not in good shape. It has been neglected for too long, and now it needs major repairs." Aurelio V described the problems with the church building, emphasizing the extra work required because of the church's historic status. "Of course it would be expensive to undertake the necessary repairs. So I have a proposition for you. I will renovate the church, entirely at my own expense, if the Archdiocese will sell me this twenty-acre parcel." Aurelio rolled out a map and showed the Archbishop the property he wanted to buy. "I am willing to pay the fair market price, so you will not lose any money on the land—plus, you'll get the church restored at no cost."

"What do you intend to do with the land?" asked the Archbishop.

Aurelio was ready for this question. He felt like the devil himself whispering into the ear of the Archbishop. "I want to build a new facility with a Christian focus that will attract families to Maravilla and to the church." It smelled fishy to the Archbishop who could spot a swindler. But he had no plans for that parcel of land, and he sure could use the money.

The Archbishop was about to ask, "What sort of facility?" But then he decided he would rather not know. Instead, he said, "I assume you are constrained from divulging the details of your project."

With great relief Aurelio answered, "Yes, that is correct," although in fact there were no such constraints. The truth is that the Archbishop had been contemplating selling some of the land in Maravilla anyway. He needed the extra cash to add some marble statuary to the Cathedral in Santa Fe.

Ultimately, the Archbishop agreed to Aurelio's proposal. Aurelio was pleased. By this time, the claws of his idea had sunk deep into his mind and wouldn't let go. Besides, it would cement his name in history along-side Aurelio I. Attorneys for the Archdiocese and Aurelio V made the legal arrangements. Finally, Aurelio called the contractor and gave him the go-ahead to draw up the plans for the restoration of the church.

When the plans were complete, the contractor submitted them to the proper authorities. Because of the historic status of the church, it took longer than usual to get a building permit. Normally a few well-placed bribes would have hurried things up, but this was not a normal case. The bureaucrats brought in experts to make sure everything would be done properly. The experts called in specialists who examined everything twice and added more restrictions.

Finally, the permit was issued, and Aurelio decided it was time to go public with the news. His first step was to organize a press conference to announce the restoration of the church. Unfortunately, the name Aurelio Salazar was not familiar to most people in the media, so the press release did not generate much of a buzz. The local newspaper sent a reporter, and a high school student intern came representing a popular radio station.

Father Ignatius announced the event at Sunday morning mass, so a smattering of local residents showed up too, along with a few curious tourists. Aurelio V staged the press conference in the church courtyard. Aurelio VI had called Paloma at the store to ask her to attend. When she arrived, Aurelio VI waved for her to come stand by him.

"Good morning," Aurelio V began. "My name is Aurelio Salazar, and I am the great-great grandson of the man who built our beautiful little church. We are lucky to have a very dedicated and resourceful priest here in Maravilla. I'm talking about Father Ignatius," he said, and he stepped back so people could see the priest. Aurelio applauded Father Ignatius and then stepped back to center stage. "Several months ago, I got a call from Father Ignatius," he said, "and he explained to me that the church is in a state of disrepair, and that he was turning to me for help. Basically, he asked me to save the church from decay and restore it to its former glory. I am proud to be a descendant of the original Aurelio Salazar, and I am here today to announce that our family has decided to take on this project." He paused for applause. When no one obliged, Aurelio VI clapped lustily, and then a few others joined in less enthusiastically, wondering what the catch was.

"Thank you," said Aurelio V. "Now, as you know, we have a very historic church here. It is so historic that the government says we can't alter the building, we have to fix it the same way it was built. The Salazar family is going to do that for Maravilla, and for everyone who visits the church. When we are done, it will be like new." He paused for a moment. Paloma heard the breeze fluttering through the leaves. "Now I would like to introduce my son, Aurelio Salazar VI, who will be the project manager." Aurelio VI smiled and waved his hand in the air. "And I believe Father Ignatius would like to say a few words." Aurelio stepped back and let Father Ignatius have the spotlight.

"I would 'ust like to say 'Thang you' to Señor Salazar and his own son, also naméd Señor Salazar too." Father Ignatius spoke slowly to balance out his strong Spanish accent. "I pray for this for long time, *y* I thing it is good thing for Maravilla. Very good thing. Thang you."

"If anyone has any questions, I'll try to answer them," said Aurelio V.

"Do you have a timeline for this project?" asked the newspaper reporter.

"Actually, we are already well on our way. We've done a damage assessment, so we know what has to be fixed. We have submitted our plans, and just last week we received the necessary permits. We're ready to go. According to our contractor, it'll take about six months."

"Is the Archdiocese involved in the project?" asked the reporter.

"The Archbishop has given us his blessing," Aurelio said.

"But no money?"

"No. The Salazar family will cover the cost of the project."

The news traveled as fast as a wildfire in a dry year, and before long everyone in Maravilla knew about the renovation of the church. It was the most talked about topic at Julio's *barberia*, at Josie's Diner, and even at the Blue Chile Tavern. As Paloma had predicted, people were thrilled. But that was before they knew about the theme park.

Aurelio V had decided to call it "Gloryland." Every game, every ride would have a Biblical reference, from the Nativity to the Resurrection: the House of Miracles, Satanic bumper cars, the Ferris Wheel to Heaven. Cars would park at Gloryland. When visitors were finished with the amusement park, they could walk to the church on a path covered with plastic palm fronds. They would marvel at the beautifully restored chapel, say a prayer, light a candle, visit the Cross of Holy Air, see the discarded crutches and canes, and finally walk across the road to the Visitors Center and Gift Shop, which would be built where the old Salazar house now stood. Aurelio decided to add a coffee shop to the Visitors Center, a place where weary tourists could sit down and have some refreshments before walking back to the car. He could offer package deals that would include tickets for rides, games and snacks.

Rising out of the Maravilla Valley, the distant mountains come into view, 14,000 feet high, snow-covered most of the year. Aurelio V bought a parcel of land overlooking that scenic view, and planned to build a pullout for tour buses. It was irresistibly photogenic.

The funeral business had made the Salazar family wealthy, and Aurelio V had enough capital and credit to work on all three projects at one time: the church, the Visitors Center and Gloryland, the theme park. He asked his attorney to incorporate a new company in New Mexico, named Gloryland, Inc. He began researching amusement park rides. He also obtained easements for the path between the parking lot and the church. This was a delicate part of the project. Aurelio negotiated with each landowner separately, explaining to them as little as possible about his plans—only that he would be building a parking lot nearby and wanted to have a path between there and the church. By now, Aurelio V was widely admired and respected for restoring the church with his own money, so most of the nearby landowners were receptive to his request for an easement. Some of them gave him the easement without charge.

Construction activity started to ramp up the very next week. One crew of workers arrived to begin the church restoration and another to tear down the old Salazar house. At the same time, at Aurelio V's new property, a sign went up in front of the site: "Coming soon: Gloryland, a Christian Amusement Park."

The sign bothered Jake. The words "Christian" and "amusement" didn't belong together in his mind. He began asking his neighbors if they knew anything about this new development. No one did. Next he contacted the planning department at Rio Grande County and learned that a company called Gloryland, Inc. had bought some land from the Archdiocese and was going to put in a new business there. The registered business agent was Aurelio Salazar V of Denver.

Jake went to see Pilar. He didn't know Pilar well, but he knew she was a leader in the community and that she had mobilized the movement to save the post office.

"Mrs. Medina," he said, "what do you know about this new development down the road called Gloryland?"

"Nothing, but I don't like the sound of it. What do you know?"

"I know who's behind the project: Aurelio Salazar. He bought the land from the Archdiocese and apparently he got the county to approve the development."

"I wonder what he's got in mind," said Pilar.

What Aurelio had in mind became more clear a few weeks later when men with chainsaws arrived and began to cut down all the trees on Aurelio's new property. Backhoes dug out the stumps and bulldozers loaded the logs onto trucks that transported the timbers to the newly razed site of the old Salazar house, where they were destined to be used in the new Visitors Center.

Chapter Fourteen

When the residents of Maravilla figured out what Gloryland was going to be and who was behind it, the bloom was off the rose with the Salazar family. Whereas Aurelio's pledge to restore the church was an act of great generosity, it was not entirely altruistic, as the locals had first thought. Devout Catholic Maravillosos opposed Gloryland as a crass attempt to make money from their shrine and their Holy Air. What good would it do for the Salazars to restore the church if they were just going to use it to turn a profit? And where would that profit go? To the church? To the village? No, it would go into the pockets of Aurelio Salazar VI, who didn't even live in Maravilla.

Over the next week Pilar received a steady stream of visitors and phone calls.

"What are we going to do about this, Pilar?" people asked.

"Can he get away with this?"

"Is it legal?"

"How can we stop him?"

Pilar called Frank Abeyta at Rio Grande County and asked him the same questions.

"Mrs. Medina," said Frank Abeyta, "Mr. Salazar has complied with all the rules and regulations in our building code. The land sale was properly executed. He has dotted all his i's and crossed all his t's. Besides, I'm not sure we have jurisdiction over Maravilla anyway. You want to form your own county and the court said that you have the right to do so. I don't think you're going to get a lot of help from us in fighting Mr. Salazar."

Freddie Sanchez of Carson County was even more dismissive. "You better get to work on your county code," he said. "And here's a bit of advice: put a heavy tax on all amusement parks." He laughed heartily and hung up the phone.

As the project manager for all three projects, Aurelio VI had moved down to Maravilla and rented a house nearby. He was a constant presence at the church, at the old Salazar house and at the Gloryland site. He sourced materials and made sure that the workers had everything they needed; he kept an eye on the workers to see which ones were skilled and industrious and which ones were lazy; he met with the inspectors to be sure that everything was up to code; he kept the projects on schedule.

At first the younger Aurelio dropped by Maravilla Blessings every few days to flirt with Paloma, but after the Gloryland sign went up, Paloma seemed always to be busy with a customer, or in the back taking inventory. In fact, Aurelio noticed a distinct change in attitude among all the villagers. Before, they had been warm and welcoming, but after the work started at Gloryland they became cool and distant, nodding when he said, "*Buenos días*," but moving on without even a smile.

One day Aurelio was able to catch Paloma coming out of the store. "Paloma," he said, "what is going on? No one will speak to me. You yourself will hardly look me in the eye."

"Don't be so dense," Paloma snapped, casting a quick glance into Aurelio's eyes. "Nobody likes the idea of having an amusement park in their back yard." She looked at him again, and this time held his eyes. "Besides, it is not right for you to make money off of our church and our religion."

"But everyone will benefit, not just my family. It will bring more tourists to Maravilla. That means more shoppers in your store, more customers at Josie's Diner, more business for everyone."

"Aurelio," said Paloma, "we are grateful that you are restoring the church. But we don't want to change our lives. We like Maravilla the way it is. Who wants to live in a tourist trap?"

"Don't think of it that way, Paloma. Think of it as a way to keep Maravilla alive, a way to make it prosper and to keep it from crumbling away like your church was. This will put Maravilla on the map!"

"We don't want to be on the map. Not for having an amusement park. And what's going on where your old house used to be? People are saying that you're going to put a motel there."

"No, no, not a motel. We want to replicate the house and use it as a kind of living museum, so tourists can see how our ancestors lived."

"Five dollars for a guided tour?" Paloma pressed on. "Ten?"

"I haven't . . . that is, we haven't," Aurelio stammered.

"And I assume you will have a gift shop, won't you, competing with ours?"

Aurelio's face reddened with embarrassment, and his eyes looked down. He wanted to disappear. Paloma beat him to it. "Good bye, Aurelio," she said emphatically, turning away, her words a stinging rebuke. Aurelio slunk away like a scolded dog.

Back at his rented home, he tried to read a book but couldn't concentrate. He paced the floor. He turned on the TV and channel-surfed but found nothing to distract him. The image of Paloma's face kept appearing in his imagination, along with her voice saying, "Don't be so dense."

Aurelio knew what the problems were; he just didn't know what to do about them. One problem was he was completely infatuated with Paloma. Maybe he was in love. He only knew that he wanted to hold her hands and look into her eyes. He wanted to be near her, sit beside her, walk with her, even if they didn't speak. And he desperately wanted her to feel the same way about him, but he knew she didn't. After their last encounter, he felt she despised him.

"*Am* I being dense?" he asked himself. Didn't everyone like amusement parks and carnivals? Why did he suddenly feel like a villain rather than a hero? Maravilla had real problems: drugs and crime and poverty. Didn't people see that this was a way to change that?

Another problem was Paloma's age. She was too young for him, he told himself. He was 26, and she was 20, still in college. Next year she would attend UNM in Albuquerque, where she would meet new friends, go out on dates, maybe have a boyfriend. She had to concentrate on her studies, not on Aurelio Salazar VI. It was an impossible situation. He should just forget about her and focus on doing his job. He could almost convince himself of this, but then in his mind he would hear her bubbly laugh, and he would be right back where he started: lovesick and forlorn.

It would be wrong to say that everyone liked Paloma, because some people thought she was too sweet, too nice, too considerate, and maybe just a little bit condescending. For better or worse, Paloma was also pretty, with raven black hair rippling down her back and azulene eyes that twinkled when she smiled her most mischievous smile.

Some people resented Paloma's cheerful personality and good looks. "Why should one person be so lucky?" wondered the man with big ears and the woman with bad teeth. Her peers admired her for getting good grades while editing the yearbook and playing on the volleyball team, all in the same year. But along with the rosy aroma of admiration, there was just a whiff of envy and even an unspoken thought that, if something bad happened to Paloma, it wouldn't be the worst thing in the world. Couldn't she at least sprain an ankle?

Aurelio was not aware of Paloma's delicate place in the eco-system of Maravilla. All he knew is that he couldn't get her out of his mind, and he did not sleep well that night. In the morning he was at the worksite early. He worked hard all day and tried not to think of Paloma. On his way home that evening, he saw Paloma's red truck pulled over on the side of the road. He pulled up behind it and parked. There was no one in the cab. The gas gauge showed half a tank. No flat tires. And no Paloma.

"Hey, you!" called a voice. Aurelio looked around and realized the voice was coming from an apple tree across the road. He walked over to the tree and saw Paloma up among the branches, picking apples and putting them into a bucket. "Here, take this," she said handing the bucket to Aurelio. She climbed down. She was wearing jeans and a plaid shirt. She didn't look any less beautiful than she did in her white dress.

"Thanks," she said. "I wasn't sure how I was going to get down without dropping the bucket."

"How'd you get up?"

"Oh, I'm good at climbing trees. Not so good at getting back down."

"Yes, I feel the same way sometimes."

"This tree has the best apples in the valley," said Paloma. "Nobody prunes it or waters it, but it's my favorite apple tree. Try one."

Aurelio picked out an apple and took a bite. It was sweet and juicy. "Wow, that's a good apple," he said.

"Thought I'd make a pie."

Aurelio carried the bucket of apples to Paloma's truck and put it in back.

"You know," said Paloma, "Maravilla is like this apple tree."

"How's that?"

"Nobody takes care of it, but it still produces great apples. The best thing to do is to leave it alone."

"But then it may die before its time."

Paloma shrugged. "So might I. Or you." Paloma got into her truck. She did not want to part on those words, but her feelings towards Aurelio were like a tangle of twine, messy and mixed up, and impossible to straighten out quickly. Her anger from yesterday's encounter had abated, but she still felt upset and uncertain about the motivations of Aurelio and his father.

"Thanks for stopping," she said, starting the engine.

"My pleasure, Paloma." Aurelio, too, wanted to say something else. He desperately wanted to keep the conversation going. He wanted to tell Paloma how he felt about her, but the words wouldn't come. Perhaps he could say something clever about apples and destiny. Paloma could see Aurelio wrestling with himself, trying to find the right thing to say. In her mind, she was encouraging Aurelio to say something personal and heartfelt. Love was in the air, like the perfume of ripe apples, and both of them could smell it but neither could grasp it.

"Take care, Aurelio," was all Paloma could say as she pulled away.

Aurelio watched the red truck until it disappeared around a turn.

Chapter Fifteen

Pilar decided it was time to have another town meeting at the Blue Chile Tavern. She spoke to Red and arranged a date and time. Signs went up at the post office, the community and senior centers. The word began to circulate.

The dance hall was packed for the meeting, with people spilling out into the courtyard. Aurelio wanted to go, but he knew he would not be welcome. When there wasn't room for another body, Pilar whacked the meeting to order with her canes. It took a few moments for the boisterous crowd to quiet down.

"You all know why we're here tonight," Pilar roared, "so let's get down to it. Is there anyone here who is in favor of the carnival that the Salazar family is planning to build?"

There was silence as everyone looked around for a hand in the air. Slowly, one went up. It belonged to Victor Sandoval of Sandoval's General Store. He stood up and addressed the crowd.

"I don't really want to see a carnival in Maravilla permanently," he said. "But I just have to say that the Salazars own the land, and if there ain't no law against it, they should be able to build whatever they want. I don't want nobody telling me what I can build on my own property."

"Victor has a point," said Pilar. "Anybody want to speak to it?" A woman stood up.

"Maybe there's no law against it yet, but we can pass one, can't we? I mean, if we're going to be our own county, we can make our own laws. Right?"

"Hold on," said Pilar. "We're not Maravilla County yet. The formal vote is coming up next month. Maybe we could convince Mr. Salazar that his operation will be illegal in due time, once we get the new county up and running."

"We'd shut him down!" someone yelled.

"He wouldn't even build it!" yelled someone else.

A thick-wristed arm went up near the front and a man stood up.

"You're making a big assumption, Pilar. We may not win the election." The speaker was a barrel-chested mechanic known as Stubs. "Every registered voter in Rio Grande and Carson County is eligible to vote. A lot of them don't agree with us. We still have to convince people outside of Maravilla to vote our way, which ain't gonna be easy. So I don't think we can use that as a threat to Mr. Salazar."

"Good point, Stubs. We don't want to look like fools."

Sylvia raised her hand. Everyone had great respect for Sylvia, since she had found a way to give Maravilla its independence, so the hall got quiet so all could hear her soft voice.

"Has anyone considered the church? If we threaten to shut down Mr. Salazar's carnival, he may stop work on the church. He's not getting paid for that work, so he has nothing to lose." There were murmurs of concern.

Juan Mendoza stood up to speak. He was a tall, thin man with a deeply lined face, permanently burnished a deep brown. He spoke with authority. "If we stop the carnival, we would lose more than the church. This is an important time in the life of Maravilla. I have lived here all my life, and I can't remember another moment as important as this one. If we chase away the Salazars, we're chasing away the tourists. And if we chase away the tourists, they will go spend their money somewhere else. Are we so wealthy that we can afford to do that? No, we are not. We are poor. We have land but no money. The Salazars' carnival is a godsend for us. We should be grateful to them. Get busy on your weavings and your jewelry, make some woodcarvings, consider opening a lunch cart or a coffee booth. I say *Viva el carnaval!*"

The crowd was stunned. Many had come up in arms, ready to run the Salazar family out of town, and now one of the older men, an *anciano*, widely known and respected, a former *majordomo*, was coming out in support of the Salazars' amusement park.

Father Ignatius had been standing quietly in the back. "What do you think, Father?" asked Pilar.

"I thing dat *el carnaval es* what you call necessary evil, no? God want *la iglesia mas linda*. I thing the church will no be finish' withou' *el carnaval. Es muy importante*."

"Anyone else?" asked Pilar.

Pete Gonzales stood up. "I just can't believe what I'm hearing. I think a circus would ruin Maravilla. How many of you have been to the county fair or the state fair?" Almost everyone raised a hand. "Do you want that atmosphere every day? Do you want to *live in* a circus? Because that's what it will be like. It might bring in money, as Juan says, but at what cost? At the cost of our tranquility. When has money ever been more important to us than tranquility? I say, let's fight it!"

"With all due respect, Pete," said Pete's neighbor, Charlie Trujillo. "Not all of us are as well off as you are. You can afford to turn down the money, but some of us can't. That's all I have to say."

A thoughtful silence descended on the room. People looked around at their neighbors and friends. "So let's do this," said Pilar. "Let's divide the room in half, right down the middle here. All of you who are in favor of the carnival go to this side. All opposed go to the other side." There was a great shuffling of feet and scraping of chairs as people changed seats and rearranged the room according to their preference. When everyone was settled, half the people sat on one side of the room and half on the other.

"Looks like we got a stalemate," said Pilar. "Now what?"

Jake had been standing quietly in the back throughout the meeting and was now sitting with the people opposed to the amusement park. When no one else responded to Pilar's question, Jake stood to address the hall.

"My name is Jacobo Epstein," he said. "Most people call me Jake. I bought the house that belonged to Lupe Lopez. So I'm a newcomer to Maravilla. But I know that this is a very special place, and I would hate to see it ruined by commercial interests. I've been wondering where the Salazars are going to get water for their amusement park."

"What do they need water for?" called out someone across the aisle.

"I don't know exactly," Jake replied. "But most amusement parks have some sort of ride that requires water, and even if they don't, they would need water to drink, to wash the equipment, to clean up after the animals, to flush their toilets, and who knows what else? We don't get much rainfall . . ."

"Eight to ten inches per year," someone shouted.

"And lately, with this drought we're in, we've only been getting half that much," Jake continued. "Of course, they can dig a well, but that could drain the water table for the rest of us, if they use a lot of water. So I'm just posing the question: how much water are they going to need and where are they going to get it?" Jake sat down.

"That's a good question," said Pilar. "And what kind of water rights do they have on that property? Pete, can you check into that?"

"I'll see what I can find out," said Pete.

On this note of uncertainty and division the meeting ended. Nobody felt satisfied with the outcome; most people left with more questions than when they had arrived.

Chapter VI, in which Tai-Keiko navigates her way through a plague of spacehoppers

After her repairs, Tai-Keiko could cruise at 2.3 light years per second. At this speed she would arrive at Zeton-9 in 10 earthly hours. She had put the spacebug on auto-pilot and taken a deep nap. She was feeling good, racing for the barn, almost there. She ate the few vi-gro pellets she had left, which were starting to degrade anyway. Tai-Keiko would be glad to get out of the mini-pod and stay out of it awhile. She was feeling cramped and constricted, her legs ached, her shoulders were tight. To make up for lost time, she drafted behind a meteor that was hauling ass toward her destination.

Tai-Keiko's pulse discriminator was picking up some activity in Area 230. She couldn't tell what it was, but her flight plan took her right through Area 230. To go around it would add a good four hours to her trip. On the other hand, if there were a serious meteor belt passing by, Tai-Keiko would have to cut her speed drastically in order to thread her way through the band. She really didn't want to change her route and decided to approach the activity and see what was going on. It might not be meteors at all. Could be a disturbance in the sub-space matrix, which would only slow her down until she could reconfigure the spectral bandwidth.

Half an hour later a foreign object grazed her spacebug. Tai-Keiko identified it as a living being and calculated it to be three inches long. It had a head with antennae, a thorax, wings and legs. The diagnostic was distinctly like a grasshopper. Of course, a normal grasshopper can't live in space, so Tai-Keiko surmised that these bugs must have developed adaptive behav-

iors, such as the ability to retain oxygen indefinitely and the ability to digest small particles of repton. Some Areas are thick with repton dust which would provide enough nutrition for any living being to survive. Other Areas are void of it. Every space creature had to find a way to collect it and store it—and of course they had.

A few more spacehoppers banged off the mini-pod. They were coming more frequently now, and they started to come in bunches smashing into the pod and depositing some anti-matter mucus that attached itself to the pod, as the remnants of the spacehoppers disappeared into space. Using her wave coil, Tai-Keiko was able to cast some light about the pod, and she could then see the hoppers. She was coming into a dense field of them. It would be impossible to dodge them unless she switched to crawl mode, in which it would seem as if time had slowed down, making it possible to skirt around the clouds of hoppers. Still, it was impossible to avoid them all, and the anti-matter mucus was piling up on the pod in great wads. Eventually it would eat its way through the pod covers and breach the atmospheric zero point. All would be lost.

It was now imperative for Tai-Keiko to reach Zeton-9 on time. She had to get out of this plague of spacehoppers. She needed free space.

To Be Continued. . .

Chapter Sixteen

Jake's agent had been trying to reach him for three days without success. Jake had gotten his agent's messages, and he knew what she wanted: more chapters. Jake had made the deadline on the first three chapters. He had been a month late on the next three. Now he was two months overdue on the third batch. His telephone startled him awake at 6:00 a.m.

"Jake, hi. It's Jennifer. You're a hard guy to reach."

"Do you know what time it is here?" asked Jake.

"Sorry. Why don't you carry your cell phone? Then I could call you at a decent hour and I wouldn't have to leave you any more of those annoying messages."

"I told you, Jennifer. I don't get cell phone reception here. The nearest cell tower is twenty miles away. That's why you have to call my landline."

"Fine," she said.

The word "fine" can mean many different things, depending on the context and the speaker's tone of voice. In this case, it meant, *Whatever, you jerk. I'll use your stupid "landline." Who even* has *a landline anymore? But I'm not going to argue with you.*

Instead, she continued, in a tone that conveyed both concern and annoyance, "You don't make it easy for your agent. How am I supposed to do business when you're practically *incommunicado?"*

"I have an email address."

"That you won't give out to anyone."

"I don't want to spend my time responding to emails from people I don't want to talk to."

"Like me, for instance."

Jake didn't say anything to this.

Jennifer said, "Not that you get much email or anything else since you won't put up a website or even a Facetime page. C'mon, Jake! Work with me here."

"Well, rest assured that I'm making progress. Things are going well. Not to worry."

"You know, when I suggested you should get out of the City, I didn't mean for you to disappear beyond the pale of civilization."

"It's civilized here. It's just remote."

"Is it working? Being remote to the point of being lost in the ozone? Is it helping you write?"

"Yes, absolutely. It's really giving me the time to focus with no interruptions. It's quiet here. I only get, like, four, five cars going by."

"Per hour?"

"Per *day*, dude."

"Shit. How can you stand it? Sounds lonely."

"Not lonely. That's the great thing about it. I'm alone, but not lonely."

"Fine." There was that word again, this time meaning, *Let's just drop it. Let's move on.*

"Look, the reason I'm calling . . ."

"I know why you're calling. You want the next three chapters."

"The next six, actually. You're falling way behind, Jake, and Hosokawa is on my case. The artist is done with the first six and is waiting for more text."

"How do they look, the first six?" queried Jake to deflect Jennifer's demands.

"Great! The publicist is itching to get a buzz started in Japan. I need more story, Jake."

"And you shall have it," Jake said, confidently. "I can send you the next three chapters by the end of the week, solid. Count on it."

"Don't bother to print them out. Just send me PDFs."

"All right, all right."

"Promise me."

"I said I would."

"Promise me," Jennifer repeated.

"Sure. I promise. Okay?"

It was a promise he might not keep, but he had to say something to end the conversation.

"Good. Now. Look, Jake, what would be really good is if you could send me a synopsis of the rest of the book. They could begin to design the frames then."

"There is no synopsis, Jen. I don't know what's going to happen next. I'm making it up as I go. I'm open to suggestions."

"Great," said Jennifer, annoyed. "Well, maybe you should think about it. Writing a synopsis, I mean. If you knew what was going to happen next, it might facilitate your writing and then maybe you could meet your deadlines."

"Good try, Jen. Spontaneity is the whole point. That's where the creative spirit lives. Like a jazz solo. Or a Jackson Pollock painting. If I plot it all out ahead of time, then it won't seem real."

"What's real is the deadline schedule you signed off on."

"I didn't promise a synopsis."

"I know. I'm just saying, it might help."

"It would take up valuable time when I could be writing."

"And it would get Hosokawa off my back."

"Does he like it so far? Hosokawa."

"Most of it. He says he's editing it. He'd feel better if he had a synopsis."

"I'd rather keep him in suspense."

"Fine, whatever," said Jennifer, meaning, *We're done here.* "But get me the next three chapters this week."

"I said I would."

"Have a good day, Jake."

Jake thought he would, in fact, have a good day. He was sure of it. He had coffee on the front porch as the sun came up. Then he sat down to work.

Jake worked straight through until mid-afternoon. By then his back was killing him and he was hungry. Jake fixed himself a sandwich and went out on the *portál* to eat. It was a warm and windy autumn afternoon, and Jake watched a flurry of yellow leaves blow off the trees. Most trees had lost their leaves, but the cottonwood leaves, brown and dry, were still clinging to the branches, making a sound that reminded Jake of running water. A black car with tinted windows stopped on the road below. The car sat there a few minutes with its engine idling. Then a window opened and a hand tossed something out onto the ground before the car drove off.

Jake went down to see what the person had thrown away. It was a syringe. He picked it up and carefully put it in the trash.

He decided to walk over to the Blue Chile Tavern for a beer. As he walked through the swirling leaves, he pondered the syringe and wondered about its user. At the bar he settled in with a plastic cup of beer, then asked Red Baca, "Is there much drug use around here?"

"Oh yeah. Very much indeed."

"What sort of drugs?"

"Heroin, crack, oxy, whatever. Marijuana, of course."

"What about pharmaceuticals?"

"Pills? Uppers, downers. Oxy, like I said." Red paused and then quickly added, "I'm not in the business myself. But I hear things."

"And you know people in the business."

"I don't ask people about their business. But I'll tell you this: Maravilla is famous for its drug use. Consistently number one in the country. In a rural area, that is. Small but mighty, that's us. Number one in drug-related murders and ODs. In towns of 10,000 or less, we beat out a place in Mississippi by one murder. For awhile we had our very own major drug smuggling gang living in plain sight. They distributed all over the West, from little ol' Maravilla."

"Distributed what?"

"Black tar heroin, mostly. But also crack and pills."

"From Maravilla?" Jake found it hard to believe. This was a side of Maravilla he hadn't seen.

"Yeah. They moved into a house on a dead-end road. Other side of the river, rickety bridge. Very inconspicuous. Just a house with a two-car garage. They had set up an operation in the garage, to break down the drugs and package them in smaller sizes. State-of-the-art security system."

"Where are they now?"

"In prison, mostly. The narcs nailed 'em. They found out about it somehow and staged a raid just before dawn: pistols drawn, warrant in their pocket. All the feds and the local cops showed up, armed and dangerous. Even a SWAT team. And the feds confiscated an arsenal of weapons."

Red was silent then, and Jake waited to hear about the shoot-out. Finally, he had to ask. "So, what happened? Anyone get killed?"

"No deaths. Coupla guys got shot in the leg, including a cop. There were eight of them, and most of them were sound asleep, so they were easy to round up. The biggest surprise was that the buildings burned down. They called it arson and laid it on one of the gang members, but I think the feds did it. Burned it to the fucking ground!"

He paused, remembering the ashes smoldering on the other side of the yellow crime scene tape. Strips of charred metal jabbed the air. Melted plastic chairs, once white, slouched in black heaps. Red had felt the heat radiating out from it and smelled the acrid stink of burned chemicals.

In Maravilla, where the very air was holy? Jake was stunned. How could it be?

"Did they used to come in here? The gang members, I mean."

"Sometimes they did. They'd sit over in that corner booth," Red pointed to the largest booth in the bar, "and drink beer, and talk. Kept to themselves. Tipped good."

"But good riddance, huh?" he asked Red.

"Oh, yeah. They were bad to the bone, the pus in an infection, and I hope they never come back. Unfortunately, they left their junkies here."

"How can people afford the drugs?" asked Jake. "There's not a lot of money here."

"This is true. It is not cheap to be a drug addict. People cut back on clothes or entertainment, even food. If that don't work, they steal. They go for the electronic gear and tools and shit. Expensive stuff that's easy to fence and hard to trace."

"And cash."

"Of course. Cash and stash. They try to pick houses where no one is home, but if they make a mistake . . ." Red drew his finger across his neck. "Dead men tell no tales."

"I got hit once when I was still in bed," Red continued. "Yeah, still in bed with my wife at six in the morning, when I hear this crack and crash, and I get up to see what the hell, in my underwear, you know, and this kid, couldn't have been more'n seventeen, eighteen come busting in waving a knife. He wore a bandana that covered his nose and mouth. I ran back to the bedroom to get my gun. He followed me, shouting at me to stop.

"'I'm from the Mexican Mafia,' the guy says, although he didn't sound a bit Mexican.

"'What the hell is the Mexican Mafia?' I ask. 'You know, he says. It's the fuckin' Mafia. In Mexico.' He made some circles with his knife, menacing, like. 'They don't have the Mafia in Mexico,' I say. 'They have cartels.' Guy gives me a look. 'Shut the fuck up,' he says. 'What do you know about it? Lie down on the bed, face down. Don't say nothing.' We lay down on the bed like he said to. I couldn't get to my gun. 'Now, I don't want to hurt you,' he says. 'I just need some money. Where's your wallet?' I say, 'In my pants, I think.' He motions with the knife. 'Get it,' he says. My pants were hanging over a chair, and I got up and pulled my wallet out of the pocket. 'How much money you got in there?' he says. I counted my money. 'Sixty-three dollars,' I say. 'Give ita me,' he says, snapping his fingers. But there was something about this guy that didn't scare me. So I say, 'I'll split it with you.'

"'What are you, crazy?' he says. 'I'll keep twenty and give you forty-three,' I say. 'That's two-thirds for you.'

"'I know that,' he says. 'You think I don't know what a third is?' he says.

"'I'm just sayin'. You're getting most of it.' We all heard a car horn honking down on the road. 'Oh, for Chrissake. All right. Gimme the forty-three,' he says. I hand him the money. The car honks again. 'I gotta go,' says the guy. 'Don't call the cops or you're a dead man. I'm sorry I busted your door.'

"Then he ran out the front door. The frame was all splintered," said Red. "I heard him climb over the gate, then I heard a car door slam, and they took off. He didn't even steal nothing else besides the money and my driver's license."

"That's a crazy story, man," Jake said. "He needed drug money, you think?"

"Probably. He was pretty hyper, like he was coming down from something."

"Or maybe it was some kind of gang initiation."

"Maybe he was scared."

"Oh, he was scared all right, but he wasn't scared of me. I think that monkey on his back scared him."

Chapter Seventeen

A special election was set up for the following March to vote on whether or not to create Maravilla County as a separate and independent jurisdiction. Proposition 1, as it was known, would be the only item on the ballot. The necessary and proper paperwork had been filed; the requisite number of eligible voter signatures had been submitted, then checked and double-checked. Surveys had been done and lines had been drawn, not without skirmishes along the way. The ballot measure read simply: "Shall create a new county, to be called Maravilla County, redrawing the Rio Grande and Carson County lines to accommodate this change, effective two years from this date." The fine print contained the exact survey lines that would define the new boundary.

Rio Grande and Carson Counties were not about to let Maravilla go without a fight, given its water reservoir and promising tourist economy. The Commissioners and the county attorneys held closed-door meetings late into the night to discuss the issue and decide what to do. They brought in the State Engineer to determine whether a new county would have any water rights. They talked to the utility companies about placing surcharges on gas and electric lines that would have to pass through the two existing counties to feed the new county. They brought in the State Historian to explain why Maravilla had been split in the first place. No one was surprised that it had been a political decision made in 1892 when the county lines were first being drawn. Politicians from both counties wanted Maravilla, so they compromised by splitting it down the middle. Since Maravilla was an unincorporated area whose boundaries were vague and undefined, the citizens never had a voice in the matter.

Over the years, the split had caused problems for both counties: problems with jurisdiction, with public services, with taxing authority, and with voting (some people managed to vote in both counties). The simplest solution would have been to redraw the lines so that Maravilla was all in one county or the other. But neither county was willing to give up its share of the tax base, for which it provided meager services. They tried to come up with a formula that would compensate the losing county, but no one trusted that any formula would be fair. And how could they be sure that compensation would be paid promptly and completely? In ten years? In twenty years? Politicians come and go, times change, and formulas are altered.

So the Commissioners for both counties agreed that they would prefer to maintain the status quo, and the only way to do that was to defeat Proposition 1.

Eligible voters for this ballot measure included not only residents of Maravilla but all registered voters in Rio Grande and Carson Counties. The Commissioners thought they could count on most voters outside Maravilla to vote against Prop 1. Even if every voter in Maravilla voted "Yes," they should be easily out-voted by the rest of the two counties. It was, they reasoned, more important to get out the vote than to convince the voters to vote "No." The logic of this did not escape the residents of Maravilla. How could they convince voters outside of Maravilla to vote "Yes" on Prop 1?

Pilar, Pete Gonzales, the Mendoza brothers, Victor Sandoval, Charlie Trujillo and a few others met to thrash it out.

"Most people vote out of self-interest," said Pete. "We need to think of reasons why it would benefit people to vote 'Yes.' Besides free beer." Everyone sat in thoughtful silence.

"We must make a list of all the bad things we can think of about Maravilla," said Horacio Mendoza. "If only we can convince people that this is a horrible place, they might say 'Good riddance' to us."

"Bad things, like what?"

"Well, we're infested with gophers, and a *chupacabra* lives near the church."

Pete rolled his eyes and silence descended again.

"We need a slogan," Pilar said.

"Free Maravilla. Vote 'Yes' on 1," volunteered Victor.

"No, not Free Maravilla, but *Dump* Maravilla," Pete said. "We have to paint ourselves as outsiders, as criminals and dope fiends. We have to run a negative campaign—against ourselves."

There was a pause while this odd idea sunk in. When it had, people started shouting out ideas. Paloma scribbled them down with a marking pen on a big pad of paper on an easel.

"Maravilla: a Hell of a Place to Live. Vote 'Yes' on 1."

"Maravilla and Drugs: a match for the Ages."

"Maravilla: #1 in murders, #1 in ODs. Vote 'Yes' on 1."

"We know where you live. Vote 'Yes' on 1."

"Maravilla: Who needs them? Vote 'Yes' on 1."

"Maravilla: where everyone is poor."

Each of these suggestions contained a grain of truth and was greeted with sardonic laughter—except for the last one, which shut everybody up.

"Scare tactics. The politics of fear," said Pilar. "Risky business. Could backfire. We might end up chasing off the tourists too."

"This all started because of the post office," said Charlie, standing up. "Is that still our main concern? If we can get the Commissioners to help us keep our post office, maybe we can forget about being our own county. It will be a lot of work to run a county. Who's going to do it?"

"Now Charlie, don't get wussy on us here." Pilar gave him the eye. "We gotta stick together," she said fiercely. "The way it works is, land-owners and tourists pay taxes to the county, and the county *hires* people to do the work. Even the Commissioners get paid. It's not a volunteer organization."

"Don't patronize me, Pilar. I'm saying it's a long haul from here to having commissioners and office workers and garbage collectors and cops." Charlie sat down.

Some of the ideas put forth that afternoon had merit; some did not. But the outcome of the special election had nothing to do with those strategies or slogans. It had to do with a basketball game.

It so happened that the state high school basketball tournament was scheduled for the same week as the election. High school basketball was a passion in northern New Mexico. Win or lose, it was much more popular than any other sporting event, amateur or professional. Rivalries between schools went deep, and the deepest of all was that between the Kit Carson Trappers and the Rio Grande Dust Devils. Both schools had had good teams in the past, but it had been twenty years since one of them played for the state championship.

The Dust Devils and the Trappers were in the same league and played each other twice during the regular season. They had split those games this year, each team winning on its home court. Both schools had good teams; each lost only one other game during the season, and they ended the season tied for first place with identical records of 18-2. To determine which team would represent the league at the state championship tournament, state officials decided the two teams would face each other in a playoff game. The game would be added to the tournament schedule and played two days prior to the first game of the state tournament. The tournament started on a Thursday, so the playoff game was scheduled for Tuesday. The winner would represent the league in the tournament; the loser would go home. No one realized that they had scheduled the playoff game for the same day as the Special Election.

Chapter VII, in which Tai-Keiko is chased around the Milky Way

The Krossarian High Command was desperate to intercept the Formula. They stepped up their surveillance of the routes to Zeton-9. Tai-Keiko became the object of a grand tiger hunt, so she eschewed her usual byways, sticking to the back ways and short cuts she remembered from earlier years. Tai-Keiko had trained as a cadet in this Area, and she knew every space hollow and backdoor route in the neighborhood.

As she approached Zeton-9, Tai-Keiko relayed her security code to the guards and was directed to an exclusive landing area. Once she was on the ground, Tai-Keiko was rushed to the Palace and asked to see Commander Fallback. She would speak to no one else. Fallback was on an overnight mission to Area 67 to mediate a dispute. Tai-Keiko explained the urgency of the situation, because of the contamination and potential breach of the atmospheric zero point. Completion of the mission required Tai-Keiko to deliver the quantum-chip to Commander Fallback only. The following day, after a restless and uncomfortable night, Tai-Keiko again presented herself to the Palace Guard and asked to see Commander Fallback. He had returned late the prior night and was still asleep.

Asleep! What a pathetic excuse if the chip breached Tai-Keiko's skin. The whole galaxy, perhaps the universe itself, would suffer greatly for so little a thing: oversleeping. Yet it wasn't long before Fallback woke and asked for Tai-Keiko to be shown in.

"Colonel Tai-Keiko," he said, "I am overjoyed to see you, for you contain the key to our survival. Are you well? Is the Formula safe?"

"Yes, Commander, all is well, but the chip must be removed immediately. It is in danger of breaching the atmospheric zero point. It could cause a galaxy-wide weather event, perhaps solar winds blowing outside their normal parameters, with a subsequent shift of planets."

"By all means. Business first." He pushed a button that summoned a doctor and nurse who beamed the chip out of Tai-Keiko's wrist into the intelligence vault. This was done in a matter of moments, and Tai-Keiko breathed a sigh of relief. The nurse also applied some anti-anti-matter cream at the spot where the chip had been implanted.

"You have done well, Tai-Keiko," said the Commander.

"Thank you, sir. I am honored to serve the Alliance."

"I assume you would like to return to Earth for some well-deserved rest."

"Yes, sir."

"I will arrange an escort to accompany you to the closest portal. We have discovered a new wormhole that the Krossarians do not yet know about. That will take you to the Milky Way galaxy, and from there you'll be home in no time."

"Thank you, Commander."

The next day, Tai-Keiko was given a new spacebug, which performed like a dream compared to the beaten and battle-scarred bug she had arrived in. Three fighter drones guarded her on her journey to the wormhole. In a thrice she was through the wormhole and back to the Milky Way. She set a course for Earth and fell into a deep slumber.

Tai-Keiko was awakened by an alarm signaling the approach of unknown objects. Her radio crackled and a voice said, "Citizen Tai-Keiko, maintain your current velocity and prepare to be vortexed."

Tai-Keiko did not know who was chasing her—perhaps the Krossarians out for revenge, or perhaps she had intruded into an Area that had been recently invaded or captured. In any case she did not intend to be vortexed by this unknown foreign legion. She immediately increased her velocity and began evasive maneuvers. She knew the Milky Way like a child knows his back yard; she knew places to hide and exposed places to avoid. When she got a bit closer to Earth, she could request a fighter ship escort, but she had a ways to go before she could do that.

Her pursuers were chasing her in a large and clumsy ship. It was powerful but did not have the flexibility for sudden changes in speed or direction that Tai-Keiko had. A missile streamed by the spacebug, narrowly missing Tai-Keiko's small ship. Another followed, clipping her wing. Tai-Keiko braked suddenly and her pursuers flew by her before they had time to react. Tai-Keiko changed course again as the giant fighter ship slowly wheeled around.

This deadly game of tag continued for the next few hours, Tai-Keiko dodging danger with her daring-do, doggedly followed by her pursuers. At last Tai-Keiko reached the Earth's solar system, but her pursuers did not fall back as she expected they would. They stayed hot on her tail. Tai-Keiko contacted her Earth base and requested a fighter escort, describing the enemy ship.

"Roger. Launching escort from Mercury," came the response.

The fighters arrived quickly but had been tracked by the enemy who destroyed the first two fighter planes. Using their debris as cover, Tai-Keiko skirted Mercury and headed for Earth. Her pursuers had to give Mercury a wide berth to avoid a collision, which gave Tai-Keiko enough time to hide behind Mars before sprinting to Earth. The enemy immediately dispatched a fleet of small fighter planes that fired on Tai-Keiko, even as Tai-Keiko executed serpentine maneuvers to evade them. Tai-Keiko took one quick turn around the Earth and determined the safest and most beautiful place to land was in North America, in a place called Maravilla. She was right about it being beautiful. She was wrong about it being safe.

To Be Continued . . .

Chapter Eighteen

The restoration of the church was completed in November, when the ground had frozen for the winter and the acequia was dry. The heavy front doors had been repaired and re-hung. A handsome iron cross stood atop the entry tower. Archie Archuleta had made the cross for nothing, just the cost of materials, and he took great pride in having his work featured so prominently. He had not been able find the metal he wanted at Ernie's Machine Shop, so he stole it from a construction site he knew about. Archie charged the Archdiocese $100 for materials, figuring that was a fair price, since the metal was worth $200 and he had gotten it for free. The cross was a simple, strong design with exquisite scrollwork at the points of the cross and a circle binding the two crosspieces together.

Other than the cross, the outside of the church was plain. The inside was another story, featuring fine woodcarvings for the stations of the cross. The original stations of the cross, carved from pine, had unfortunately rotted away after 150 years in the damp, unheated church. To replace them, Aurelio asked fourteen of the finest and best-known woodcarvers in and around Maravilla to contribute one station each. The woodcarvers all knew that their work could become part of the church for hundreds of years to come. It became an unofficial competition, with each carver striving to do his best work and show off his most impressive skills. It would secure their place in the lore of woodcarving. The finished carvings were painted in delicate strokes, either by the carver or by a special *bulto* painter. The color brought light to the reliefs, defining every important fold in a garment, the deep lines in a face, or a drop of blood on the brow.

There was Mary, Jesus' mother, weeping and screeching uncontrollably, as every mother would who saw her son stabbed in the side and crucified on a cross. Jesus in return looked at his mother for forgiveness. The woodcarver sought to convey that Jesus believed he had failed his mother. He would join his Father in Heaven, but he had failed his mother on earth. He had not lived up to her rightful expectations, he had not been an attentive son. He had neglected his mother, and the carver used his knife on the wood to expose this feeling. It was a vivid and moving presentation of that tragic meeting.

Another of the outstanding *bultos* portrayed Christ stumbling and falling as he was forced to drag an enormous wooden cross for an undetermined distance—far enough to fall three times. The carver filled the face of the fallen Christ with anguish, magnifying the pathos of Christ having to wrestle His weighty burden through the hostile crowd, which was spitting on Him and throwing rocks at Him. In yet another scene Jesus was being stripped of his garments in preparation for crucifixion, and in the background the carver had depicted four fierce Roman soldiers ready to nail Christ to the cross. The fourteen *bultos* were powerful representations of Christ's procession to Calvary, and any one of them could make a pilgrim weep.

The eleventh station was especially gruesome. The lucky man who drew that assignment was a 78-year old carver named Eduardo Estrada. He was renowned for his rendering of particularly violent and bloody scenes, and he outdid himself for the Cross of Holy Air. Blood was everywhere, oozing from the crown of thorns on Christ's head and dripping off his hands and toes from the spikes driven into his feet, with plenty more blood gushing from the sword wound in his side.

For the main crucifix, a *bulto* mounted behind the altar, Aurelio decided to keep the original. It was made of hardwood and had not deteriorated. It was exquisitely carved and only moderately gory.

Of all the improvements the Salazars made to the church—repairing the walls, replacing the roof, cleaning the ceiling—Aurelio VI was most pleased by the new carvings of the stations of the cross. He was tempted to illuminate the stations with candlelight—electric light was not allowed because of the church's historic status—but the idea of fire being so close to the carvings worried him, and he decided against it. Light entered the room through a border of small windows high on the walls. Enough light filtered down to eye level, he decided, to allow pilgrims to appreciate the artistry inherent in the stations.

The last task to complete the renovation of the Cross of Holy Air Catholic Church was to whitewash the outside walls. Father Ignatius hoped the entire community would participate in this event. He picked a date—a Saturday in early December—and began to advertise it around. From the pulpit he encouraged people to come. He put up flyers in all the stores nearby and persuaded a paint company in Santa Fe to donate the whitewash and brushes.

The day dawned clear, sunny and cold. Father Ignatius stacked the buckets of whitewash just outside the courtyard. He had borrowed ladders from the volunteer fire department. His plan was to start at 10:00 in the morning and go until they were done, hopefully before dark. Josie and Dennis Duran supplied vats of hot coffee and apple muffins from Josie's Diner. People started arriving early and kept coming in a steady stream. By the time Father Ignatius rang a bell for attention, about fifty people were there, stomping their feet to keep warm.

"*Buenos dias mis amigos y vecinos*. I am gla' to see you all. I am exciting you are here. Thang you for to come." He began to open the paint cans and hand out brushes. Before long people had created a system to keep the painting process orderly, so that the whole building got covered, but no one got paint splattered onto their heads.

Not all the volunteers were Catholics. Red showed up and so did Archie. They were agnostics. Jake was there, a Jew by upbringing. Lots of Presbyterians came to help out. Catholic or not, Maravillosos were proud of the renovated church and wanted to lend a hand.

By late afternoon, the sun was setting and the job was done. Two coats of whitewash had been applied, and the church gleamed in the late afternoon light. It was a jewel of a church that would serve Maravilla for generations to come.

That night was dark and cold, with only a sliver of a moon. The next morning, the sun rose in an icy blue sky. It was a pale, gentle blue that infused the sky in Maravilla in the winter months. It was not the deep heartbreaking blue of summer—neither the turquoise on a close horizon nor the bright sapphire blue in the distance—but a soft azure blue that gleamed with the clarity of a diamond.

Father Ignatius expected to have a large congregation for Sunday's ten o'clock mass, and he did. Many of them had been there the day before, helping to whitewash the church. Others came too, wanting to witness a local happening, an event of some importance to the community that would remain in the collective memory for years—the first mass in the renovated Cross of Holy Air Catholic Church.

But when the first of the flock arrived, they were greeted not by a beautiful, pristine church, white as a dove, but by four white church walls that had been thoroughly tagged in the black and red spray paint of graffiti vandals. The tags were, as usual, stylized and impossible to decipher, enigmatic symbols shouting out against the white wall of purity, demanding that attention be paid to them, not to buildings, not to gods, not to goods, not to anything but themselves.

Was it destructive behavior or a plea for help? If it was the latter, the vandals did not make it easy to help them.

This was not the first time graffiti vandals had defaced property in Maravilla—far from it. Walls, fences, fire hydrants, mail boxes, road signs, large rocks—almost everything seemed to be fair game. The property owners swore in frustration, and then either painted over the tags or scrubbed them off with paint remover, only to be defaced again a few weeks later. The vandals worked at night and struck quickly. No one ever saw them, to say nothing of catching them. But to hit the newly painted church with their ugly scribblings—this was the last straw. Something had to be done.

A few days later, Pilar Medina hoisted herself into her car, met up with Father Ignatius at the church and drove from Maravilla to Rio Grande High School. They found the principal's office and waited while the receptionist finished a phone call. The principal, Mrs. Flora Chavez, was a small woman who exuded an air of calm strength. She was in a conference with the family of a boy named Jesús Sanchez, an eleventh grader who had stolen some chemicals—hazardous chemicals—with the intent of selling them to a drug dealer who knew a guy who had a source who would buy these chemicals. Jesús was a good student, especially in chemistry, but he was always broke and wanted to have a smart phone. Jesús's parents were not stingy, just poor, with three other kids at home. The boy's father worked at an auto parts store. They didn't have enough money to buy a phone for Jesús. It was one of those situations that people can only shake their heads about, because life is not fair and yet everyone is supposed to follow the same rules. All they knew for sure was that stealing from the school was wrong. It was complicated by the fact that Jesús was doing well in school, getting good grades and staying out of trouble—until now. If he graduated, he would be the first in his family to do so. Mrs. Chavez was in a quandary because she wanted Jesús to succeed in school, but she couldn't let his crime go unpunished.

Pilar asked to see the principal. The receptionist explained that Mrs. Chavez was dealing with a difficult situation and it would take awhile.

"We'll wait," said Pilar.

Seating in the outer office area was limited. Against one wall there was a two-person couch, covered with pale green fake leather, and against the opposite wall stood a hard-backed chair next to a small table strewn with magazines and leaflets. Pilar subsumed the couch, and Father Ignatius sat on the chair, feeling as out of place as a ballerina at a bull-fight. Neither of them talked, choosing instead to listen to the teenaged chit-chat that came and went in the office.

"I need a late pass, Miss Debbie," said one girl to the receptionist.

"Why are you late?" asked Miss Debbie.

"I missed the bus and had to walk down to the state road to hitch-hike to school."

"You shouldn't hitch-hike, Sabrina. It isn't safe."

"Well, then I would have gotten here even later."

Miss Debbie handed her a slip of paper and Sabrina went off to class.

One boy was hauled in for fighting, and Miss Debbie told him to stand in the corner and be quiet.

Finally, Mrs. Chavez opened the door to her office and the young thief left with his parents. Miss Debbie went in the principal's office and closed the door.

"There are two people from Maravilla to see you," she said.

"Parents?"

"I don't think so. One is an older woman and one is a priest."

"Okay, show them in."

Pilar hobbled in on her canes; Father Ignatius followed, looking at the floor with his hands folded.

"I'm Flora Chavez. What can I do for you?" asked Mrs. Chavez.

Pilar explained about the tagging of the church. She showed the principal several photos of the church walls covered with hieroglyphic tags. "We'd like to find out who did this," said Pilar, "and we thought maybe you had seen some of these marks before, and maybe you even know who they belong to."

Mrs. Chavez studied the photos. "Yes," she said, "I recognize some of these tags, but I don't know whose they are. Have you talked to the police?"

"Yes. They were sympathetic, but not very helpful."

"Do you have any reason to think the vandals go to school here?"

"No, except that taggers tend to be teenaged boys."

"True, but they could be drop-outs or gang members from another town."

Pilar pulled out a business card and handed it to the principal. "Here's my card from my store. You can reach me there if you think of anything."

"I will do that. Can I keep some of those photos? They might be useful."

"Of course." Pilar gave her four shots of the graffiti.

Later that day Mrs. Chavez had an idea. She called Jesús Sanchez to her office. She spread out the photos on her desk. "Jesús, do you recognize these tags?" she asked.

The boy looked at them carefully. "Maybe," he said.

"Who do they belong to?"

"I can't tell you that."

"Because . . ."

"Because I won't rat out a friend of mine."

"So, the tagger is a friend of yours?"

"Not exactly. But he's a, what do you call it? A peer."

"So stealing from the school is okay, but ratting out your peers is not?"

Jesús didn't respond to this question.

"Let's try this," said Mrs. Chavez. "I'll ask you some questions, and you answer yes or no. You don't have to give me any names. Okay?"

Jesús shrugged.

"Does the tagger go to school here?"

"No."

"Did he used to go to school here?"

Jesús bit his lip and nodded.

"Did he graduate?"

"No."

"Drop out?"

"Yeah."

"Was he in your class?"

Jesús nodded.

Mrs. Chavez got out a yearbook that was two years old. "Would he be in this yearbook?"

"Maybe. I don't know."

"Okay. I'm going to go through the pictures of your class, and I want you to stop me when I get to the page with his picture on it."

"Mrs. Chavez, this is . . ."

"Jesús," the principal interrupted, "you are in big trouble and I haven't decided what to do about it yet. But I assure you, if you cooperate with me, it's likely I will be more lenient than if you don't."

Jesús sighed. He was only trying to get a cell phone, and it had led to this. "This sucks," he muttered. The principal pretended not to hear him.

"Here we go," she said.

There were 159 students in Jesús's freshman class. Mrs. Chavez faced the yearbook toward Jesús and turned the pages slowly. After six pages, Jesús said, "Stop."

"He's on this page?" the principal asked.

"Yeah."

"Okay. Thank you. I won't ask for more—unless you'd like to identify the tagger for me."

Jesús shook his head. "Can I go now?" he asked.

"Yes, you may go. I appreciate your cooperation. And Jesús, this is just between you and me. I won't . . . rat you out."

There were pictures of 12 male students on that page, and Mrs. Chavez identified three who had since dropped out of school. She called a friend of hers in the sheriff's office, a lieutenant, and explained that she had three suspects for the church tagging in Maravilla, whose tags had also shown up numerous places around the area, including schools, businesses and public property. She asked him to investigate.

"Flora, I don't have time to run down taggers. I've got two burglaries and a homicide on my desk."

"Look, my friend. Everyone complains about graffiti, but no one does anything about it. Here's your chance. Just make a few phone calls and maybe a home visit or two, that's all I'm asking."

The lieutenant sighed. "Do you have photos of the tags?"

"Yes. I'll scan them and email them to you, along with pictures of the three suspects and their names."

"Oh, all right. I'll get back to you."

The lieutenant quickly found out that the first suspect had moved away with his family six months earlier. The second suspect, named Carlos Delgado, wasn't home, and his mother didn't know where he was. The third suspect, a seventeen-year-old named José, was flipping burgers at Bueno Burgers and was clearly nervous when the policeman asked to talk to him. They went into the office in back. The lieutenant spread out the photos.

"Which one of these tags is yours?"

"None of them. I don't do that no more."

"Do you recognize this tag?" asked the cop, pointing to the most prominent tag.

"It's not mine," said the boy.

"I didn't ask you that. Do you recognize it?"

"I've seen it around."

"Whose is it?"

"I don't know."

"Do you like your job, José?"

"It's okay."

"You wanna keep it?"

"I didn't do nothing wrong."

"Hey, it's wrong to withhold information from a police officer. Tell me whose tag this is, and I'll tell your boss you're clean. Your other choice is to come down to the station and we'll talk some more. I can't guarantee you'll still have a job after that."

"Shit. If I finger him, he'll beat the crap out of me."

"This is just between you and me."

José looked down at the floor. "Carlos Delgado," he said quietly.

"Carlos Delgado. Good. Thank you. You know where I can find him?"

"No, but he hangs out at the skateboard park a lot."

"Okay, one more thing. Were you involved in tagging the church in Maravilla?"

"What? No, man. I didn't have nothing to do with that."

"What if Carlos says you did?"

"Then he's a liar. I ain't been out tagging since I got this job."

"That's good, José, that's good. But if I find out you're lying to me. . ." He let the sentence hang.

"I ain't lying, man."

"Okay. Then we're done here."

The police lieutenant drove to the skateboard park and identified Carlos Delgado from his yearbook picture. The officer stepped up to Carlos.

"County Police," he said. He put his mouth uncomfortably close to Carlos's face. His breath smelled of onions and chile.

"Wait, hold on. I didn't do nothing wrong."

"I've heard that song before, Carlos. Just get in the backseat. These things hurt, believe me." He dangled the cuffs in front of Carlos' face.

The sheriff's deputy put his hand on Carlos's head to protect it as he pushed Carlos into the back seat of the police cruiser.

"You've got two choices, Carlos," the lieutenant said, once Carlos was seated in back. "You can admit that you tagged the church in Maravilla. In that case, you clean off the tags and I'll drop the charges. Or we can go to court, where you'll lose and have to spend a couple of months in jail. Plus, you'll still have to clean off the tags on the church wall."

"Aw, man!"

"Maybe you should get some of your friends to help you. Cleaning that wall is a big job. Gonna take some time. I want it done by Christmas."

Ultimately, Carlos chose the first option. And thus the walls at the Cross of Holy Air Catholic Church were made white again, just in time for Christmas.

Chapter Nineteen

Aurelio VI was driving back to Maravilla from Santa Fe after a quick trip to town for a bag of stucco in a custom color that he wanted to try out on the Visitor's Center. Aurelio liked to run unexpected errands such as this. It gave him a chance to escape the more or less constant barrage of questions to answer, decisions to make, and changes to consider. Once Aurelio got off the main highway on the return trip, he always enjoyed the spectacular ten-mile drive through rugged rocky country, a landscape of red sandstone nearby and blue Jemez mountains in the distance. These were the *barrancas*, the badlands, whipped by the wind, drowned by sudden deluges, baked under a scorching sun.

Aurelio saw a man walking on the shoulder in a crooked line, a beer in one hand despite the chilly January day. He trudged forward with his thumb stuck out. Aurelio did not normally pick up hitchhikers. The possibility of foul play was too present to ignore. Who knows what a desperate man in a desolate land would do?

Aurelio picked him up anyway. This character didn't look very dangerous to him. He looked like someone who needed a break. He stopped in front of the man, and waved at him to come get in. In his rearview mirror, Aurelio watched the man approach. It was a familiar face: Aurelio had seen him around Maravilla.

"Thanks, boss," said the hitchhiker opening the truck's door. "It's friggin' cold out there." He secured his beer, heaved himself up and slammed the door. "Name's Archie."

"Aurelio Salazar."

Aurelio pulled back onto the road. "I'm only going to Maravilla," he said.

"Perfect. That's where I'm headed," said Archie. "I live there. Say, aren't you the guy that . . . don't you own . . . aren't you the one who's building the new house? And fixing up the church?"

"That's me. Me and my family."

"The Salazar family."

"That's right."

"Well, here's to you, bro'," said Archie, lifting his beer in a toast.

"Thanks." He forced himself to say, "We want to do our part to improve the community."

"Right on, man. Tha's very noble." Aurelio heard the slight alcoholic slur in Archie's words. "So what do you do in Maravilla?"

"Oh, this and that. I work for this guy Pete Gonzales, you know him?"

"We've met. What do you do for him?"

"I help him out around his farm. And I do a little metalwork on the side."

"Oh, yeah? Like jewelry?"

"No. More heavy duty stuff. Welding work, wrought iron, you know. I make window grates, and gates and crosses. Whatever. I'm the guy who made the new cross on top of the church."

"Oh, yes, I remember now. Beautiful work!" Archie smiled and blushed. He didn't think of his welding as "work."

Further north, the Truchas peaks gleamed with snow. A tumbleweed as big as a truck tire blew by them. Aurelio turned onto the road to Maravilla, which descended from the barren *barrancas* down into the river valley, flush with trees, lushly green in the summer but gray this time of year.

Archie drained his beer and crushed the can under his boot. He put it in his jacket pocket.

"Home sweet home," he said. "You can just drop me at your construction site. Hey, if you need any metalwork done, let me know. I could make you a real nice gate, or maybe a candelabra for the dining room table. Whatever you need."

"Thanks, man. I'll definitely keep you in mind." Aurelio liked to hire local workers whenever possible; it helped solidify his stature as a good man who cared about Maravilla. He remembered now about Archie's drinking problem, which helped to explain what Archie was doing out in the badlands in the middle of winter with a beer in his hand.

The reconstruction of the old Salazar house was going smoothly. What had once been a proud villa had become a hazard and a decrepit wreck after decades of neglect, and only the most rabid preservationists were sorry to see it go. The bulldozers and wrecking crews took it down in two days, hauling away several trailers full of refuse to the dump. When the ground was cleared and leveled, clean dirt was brought in to be the floor of the house. A layer of dirt was spread and then compacted. This process was repeated several times until the floor was hard and smooth. A truck arrived with pallets of adobe bricks. While some workers were making mortar from mud, others were laying the bricks. The outside walls were three feet thick: a course of adobe bricks on the outside and another on the inside with ample airspace in between for insulation.

"This simple construction would keep the house warm in the winter and cool in the summer," the docent would say. Aurelio was beginning to think of a script for the guides. He read up on clothes and tools of the day, talked to architects and historians about building techniques, and to food gurus about gardens and animals and cooking.

The architect tried to remain true to the original design. He tried to reconstruct the house on paper from the ruins, memories and one sepia-toned photo from 1888. The only known photographic evidence had been taken at the ceremony when Aurelio I, a dying man, transferred the deed to the Archdiocese. In that picture, the house is in the background, across the road, with Aurelio I and the Archbishop smiling and shaking hands in the foreground. With Aurelio VI, the architect had talked to the older residents to ask them what they remembered about the house. Sometimes the photo would bring up a memory. It was a clear view of the house. It had been a sturdy two-story adobe, with a portal on each level, wrapping around one corner. The peaked roof had been made of cedar shingles. The beams holding up the portal were epic Ponderosa pine from the mountains to the east.

As the weeks went by, an impressive structure went up that had people wondering who was going to live there. This mystery was compounded when a sign appeared announcing that the building was "The Future Home of the Gloryland Visitors Center and Gift Shop."

Aurelio VI became a goodwill ambassador for the Visitors Center. He printed up a brochure that explained how the center would be a "living museum" where people could glimpse life as it was 300 years ago. Tours would be held three times a day, and the guide, wearing clothes of the period, would talk about day-to-day life as it was "back then," about the foods they ate and the tools they used. The brochure told the story of Aurelio I's discovery of the Holy Air through a dream, and how God told him to build a church on that spot. There were pictures of the house in its dilapidated condition next to drawings of the new house that was being built.

When the land for the amusement park had been cleared, the community had a mixed reaction. Some saw it as a boon, some as a bane. Aurelio V decided to finish the church and the house first, and win over the residents before he built the carnival. Besides, Aurelio VI was busy with the house and the church. He wanted to get every detail right, from the hard dirt floors to the grand portal with its corbels carved in fan patterns.

When the Visitors Center was all but finished—inspections passed and the "certificate of occupancy" posted—Aurelio VI took a careful look around to see if anything was missing or out of place. He noticed that the massive iron and steel kitchen stove had pots and pans but no utensils. He immediately thought of the hitchhiker who did metalwork. Aurelio put out the word that he was looking for a metalworker called Arnie or Artie. "Oh, you mean Archie," people said. Most admitted that Archie was a good metalworker when he was sober. "Such a waste of good talent," they would say. A few days later, Archie showed up at the building site looking for Aurelio. He wasn't holding a beer, but his breath had the sour smell of booze.

"I heard you were looking for a blacksmith," Archie said.

"Yes," Aurelio replied. "I need some iron kitchen utensils."

"Like what?"

"A large spoon, a soup ladle, a spatula, maybe a pair of tongs. . ."

"I could make those for you," said Archie. They talked about size and dimensions and cost.

"Now, Archie," Aurelio said, "I've heard that you drink a lot. Do you think you can sober up to make these for me?"

"Oh, yes, sir. I always work sober. Just ask Pilar."

"I don't want any accidents."

"Don't worry, boss. I'll be careful."

Aurelio didn't see the harm in giving him a chance. If Archie didn't deliver, he wouldn't get paid. They settled on a price and a two-week deadline. As usual, Archie asked for an advance for materials, and Aurelio fronted him fifty bucks.

As was his custom, Archie went to the Blue Chile to celebrate his commission. Red sold him a beer and a pint of whiskey, but he cautioned, "Don't screw this up, Archie. This is your legacy."

"It's just a few kitchen tools, that's all."

"You know, you could make a slew of iron spoons and sell them in the gift shop. Put one in a fancy box, and it's the perfect gift."

"I don't know, Red. Fancy boxes?"

"What you need is a partner, Archie. Someone to handle the sales and so on. Leave you to make the utensils."

"Work, work and more work. That's what it sounds like to me," Archie said.

Later on, Archie went to Ernie's Machine Shop to buy iron. He scoured the yard for pieces that would make good handles for the ladle and spoon, and other useful scraps. Ernie charged him ten bucks, and, feeling flush, Archie paid for it in full.

"What did you do? Win the lottery?" asked Ernie.

"No, but these pieces are going into a museum, so they deserve full price."

"Is that a fact? Which museum?"

"The Gloryland Museum. The old Salazar house is going to be a museum."

"Is that a fact?" repeated Ernie. "I shoulda charged you more."

The next morning Archie set alight the coals in the forge. A few hours later, when the temperature was high enough, he started working the metal, letting it heat up in the fire, then hammering it into shape on the anvil. When a piece was pounded to perfection, he doused it in a tub of water, releasing an enormous cloud of steam hot enough to take your nose off. Later, when they had cooled, Archie welded pieces together with his torch. Strictly speaking, this was cheating because the settlers did not have access to an acetylene torch. But Archie saw no sense in making a job harder than it really needed to be, just for the sake of authenticity. The logic of that argument was clear to him, and he felt no guilt. In fact, he would have felt stupid doing it the old fashioned way. *What good is technology if you don't use it?* was his position.

In the gift shop Aurelio VI was planning to sell high-end Christian jewelry: turquoise and silver bracelets and earrings featuring crosses and angels. He also wanted to sell vials for Holy Air and *milagros*, as Pilar did, but he didn't want to anger or alienate Pilar. He decided to ask Pilar to be his wholesaler for several items. He would try to keep peace between them by buying from her. He explained his proposal to her.

Pilar thought a moment before she said, "I will charge you my cost plus 10%, which is still significantly cheaper than my store price."

"I can live with that," said Aurelio.

"One other thing," said Pilar. "You can't undercut my store price. You can sell them for more but not less."

"You are hard-headed, Pilar, but I accept your conditions."

Aurelio found that local artisans who already sold to Pilar—woodcarvers, tin smiths and painters—refused to sell to Aurelio directly. They all wanted to funnel their work through Pilar. Aurelio felt this was taking it too far, and he went to Santa Fe to seek out artisans there. On the mass-produced items, he would buy from Pilar. For the one-of-a-kind pieces—*bultos, retablos* and tin work—he would compile his own stable of artists. The only exception was Archie, who was already doing work for both Aurelio and Pilar, so Aurelio felt no compunction about dealing with Archie directly for his crosses. They were very creative, clever and handsome, no two alike.

When Archie finished the kitchen tools, he took them to Aurelio who was impressed.

"These are perfect, Archie," he said. "Just what I wanted." Encouraged by Archie's work, Aurelio asked him if he would do a few jobs on the house for him. There was some welding work to do on the second floor in the caretaker's quarters. Although spartan downstairs, upstairs the Salazars had made some concessions to the modern era, such as running water, electricity and bathrooms. That is where the caretaker would live, but it was still vacant.

Aurelio asked Archie to weld some metal shelves together, a simple job. Archie borrowed Paloma's old truck to transport his welding gear to the Visitors Center. On the way there, he stopped at the Blue Chile for a beer. Jake was there, talking about the county referendum with Red.

"This thing is going all the way to the state Supreme Court," Jake predicted. "It's a constitutional matter, and it will set a major precedent, so they aren't going to let a lower court decide the outcome. It's headed to the Supreme Court."

"I heard the ACLU was interested," said Red. "Or was it UCLA? I'm not sure. But I don't think Pete is going to be our lawyer for the next round."

"Probably not, although I don't know why. I thought he did a great job."

"No shit," said Red. "Wanna beer, Arch? Stupid question." He poured a plastic cup for Archie, who jumped into the conversation. "You ask me," he said, "it's gonna be decided behind closed doors somewhere. The Governor and some judges and lawyers are gonna sit down with some Jack Daniels and decide what to do. We're just the foot soldiers, *qué no*?"

"The thing is," said Jake, "we shouldn't let them shove us aside. If it goes to the Supreme Court, we gotta get a picket line together. We gotta get organized. Then it's the little guy vs. The Government. Everyone is always for the little guy. We just have to be more aggressive than they are. We get public opinion on our side, and then we'll win."

"That is just naïve tough talk. Maybe everyone is for the little guy, but how often does he win?"

This conversation went on like this for the next hour, during which time Archie had three more beers.

"Well," he said, slapping a fiver on the bar, "I gotta go do some welding for Mr. Salazar."

"Might not be the best time to do it," said Red. "Do it in the morning, Arch."

"I'm fine," said Archie. "I do my best work with a buzz on."

Archie went out and was nearly blinded by the setting sun. He pulled on his welder's helmet, which reduced the sun to a pinpoint on the horizon. Everything else was darker too, but Archie could see fine. He drove Paloma's truck to the Visitors Center, parked by the sign and hauled his equipment up the stairs to the second floor. He tripped once but caught himself.

The caretaker's quarters were very nice for a one-person apartment. There was a living room, a bedroom, a kitchen and a roomy bathroom. Aurelio had not interviewed applicants for the caretaker job yet.

Archie set up his welding gear and went to work. He was about halfway done putting together the shelves when he heard gunshots in the distance. In Maravilla, it was not uncommon to hear a gunshot every now and then, but he heard three in a row, followed a moment later by a fourth.

Chapter Twenty

Archie hurried to the second floor window and peeked out cautiously. He saw an unusual vehicle parked in the cemetery. The top opened and a figure, in what looked like white sportswear, emerged and ran toward the church, crouching down by the wall of the church courtyard. This was odd indeed. He heard another gunshot, closer than before. What puzzled Archie most was the sound of the gunfire. The shots had not just a crack but a kind of ripping noise, like tearing a piece of cloth. He had never heard a gunshot sound like that.

A young girl in a blue dress ran across the road. A shot cracked and ripped, and the girl fell to the ground.

"Luisa!" cried a woman's voice in horror. The girl's mother ran into the road to her fallen daughter. Another shot cracked and the mother fell beside her daughter. There was no blood, Archie noticed. Perhaps their assailant was using a stun gun.

Sirens could be heard in the distance, coming closer. The figure clad in white ran past the church and took cover behind an ancient cottonwood, clearly holding a weapon of some kind. A state trooper pulled up to the church and saw the two figures lying in the road. Archie heard a whoosh and the cop car exploded into orange flames and black smoke.

The Figure in White ran behind the next building just as two extra-human-sized figures carrying weapons emerged onto the road. "What the hell?..." muttered Archie. He was looking at two Giant Creatures, each with four legs, two short arms with claws, and a scorpion-like tail that could swivel in any direction. At the end of the tail were pincers, holding what looked like a weapon. They also had retractable wings, and their eyes roamed constantly and quickly, picking up the slightest movement.

Another police cruiser arrived from the opposite direction. The officer shielded himself behind the driver's side door and opened fire on the Creatures, but the bullets had no effect on them. One fired on the cruiser, exploding it into scrap metal.

Chapter VIII, in which Tai-Keiko lands in Maravilla, pursued by Krossarians

As Tai-Keiko prepared to land, she detected a Krossarian fighter ship in the vicinity. Somehow it had penetrated Earth-Shield and was searching for her.

Tai-Keiko landed in a cemetery next to a church. She flipped open the hatch, grabbed her Laser-Luger and took cover outside the church's courtyard. Looking around at the buildings, she wondered if perhaps her ship had creased the space-time continuum. It was obvious she had landed in an earlier Earth time, possibly the early third millennium A.D., although the buildings looked a century or two earlier than that. This would explain how they had penetrated the EarthShield: because there was no EarthShield at that time. If the ozone reading was accurate, it could be as early as 2020, or even earlier.

But this was no time for archaeological musings. Her transducer detected aliens nearby. Crouching in the shadows of the church wall, she saw a girl run into the road where a gunshot dropped her like a rag doll and she lay still. Tai-Keiko saw her mother run to her, but she was also shot down. The gunshots had the distinctive sound of a Krossarian Riplash 700, which immobilized the victim until the shooter decided whether to kill or revive him . . . or her.

Tai-Keiko crept along the church wall, then ran to the shadows of a giant old cottonwood tree. She heard sirens. A state police car pulled up in front of the church and was immediately destroyed in a fiery flash by the Krossarians. Apparently, the Riplash was not the only weapon they carried. Tai-Keiko ran to the back of the next building. Two Krossarians—in the form of scorpions—swiveled into sight, stalking slowly and boldly down the road, looking for Tai-Keiko. They should know that she no longer had the Formula; maybe they were just being thorough, or maybe they were out for revenge. Tai-Keiko did not know the Formula, but torture was the only way the Krossarians could be sure.

A moment later another cop car entered the scene; the enemy quickly took it out in a billow of fire and smoke.

Ironically, Tai-Keiko did not have any of the deadly vapor to use against the Krossarian scorps, but she knew that the Krossarian scorpion had one weak point: its front underbelly. It was protected on the sides by a diamond-hard shell, but there was one vulnerable spot, on the front of the scorp just between its upper legs. It would take a frontal shot to hit it, and Tai-Keiko might be killed before she got her shot off. The only other possibility, risky at best, was to ricochet a bullet off a hard surface to penetrate the underbelly. A large boulder stood on the side of the road. The scorps were approaching it now. If Tai-Keiko missed, her position would be exposed and she would be captured or killed. But it was her only chance. She calculated the necessary angle and the proper distance. Time was running out; in a few moments they would pass the boulder. Tai-Keiko squeezed the trigger. Her shot hit the mark, and the first scorpion toppled over, its tail thrashing wildly. The second scorpion turned toward Tai-Keiko, leaving open its vulnerable underbelly. The scorp fired toward Tai-Keiko but missed as Tai-Keiko dove behind the building, shooting at the underbelly of the beast as she rolled away. The second scorpion froze when the bullet entered its body, and then collapsed in the dust. Its tail flailed in the scorp's throes of death. Tai-Keiko sliced up the scorpions' tails like carrots, then ran to her craft and made a quick exit from the scene.

To Be Continued . . .

Chapter Twenty-One

Archie saw it all from the upper floor of the Visitors Center. When the second Creature went down, he watched the Figure in White approach the Creatures cautiously, holding a gun with both hands, trained on the Creatures. From the end of the gun streamed a red beam of light that sliced through the scorpion tails. The Figure in White ran back to the cemetery, got into a small vehicle and lifted off like a silent helicopter.

Archie walked out of the Visitors Center to the road. Some residents cautiously peered out their doors. Pilar hobbled out of her store. The two dead Creatures lay in the middle of the road. Alice took pictures of the Creatures with her phone. Cautiously, more people emerged from the shops, the galleries and the church, curious rubberneckers, with stunned looks from those in front of the circling crowd. The zapped mother and daughter were beginning to stir, injured but not dead. They were given water. At either end of the road a police cruiser was burning, with an officer incinerated in each fiery car. Alice took pictures of them too.

Kids were drawn to the Creatures: the thick green blood, their gigantic size, their lifeless faceted eyes, frozen open, their tail stubs still twitching. Parents yelled at them to stay away, to get back. Many more police arrived: county, state and, eventually, the FBI. The men in charge decided the area should be evacuated. The residents—fifty or so people, including the priest—were asked to pack their bags. They would be housed, at the state's expense, at a casino hotel nearby. Pilar and Archie went home. An FBI agent was talking on the phone to his boss, trying to figure out what the hell to do. They decided to quarantine the area, secured by the National Guard, until the FBI could mount a thorough investigation. They posted armed guards around the perimeter, 24-7.

This cordoning-off brought the Salazars' projects grinding to a halt. Aurelio VI tried to get an estimate of when he could begin work again, but was told only that the investigation would take an indefinite amount of time.

In Denver, Aurelio V immediately began to scheme ways to make money off the event. He asked his son to interview everyone who was there, to see if there were any pictures, maybe a video, and also to snap some shots himself: in short, to do everything the FBI would do. So Aurelio went room to room at the hotel at the Wild Horse Casino interviewing everyone from Maravilla about the incident. He had gotten a few pictures of the Creatures before the FBI stopped him and took his camera. Luckily, Alice still had the pictures on her phone. She posted a few of them online and they went viral in 24 hours.

Thanks to Alice's photos, the major news media flew in to cover the story. Newspapers and television ran all the old news about a spacecraft landing in Roswell, New Mexico in 1947, and the possible sighting of alien beings. But unlike Roswell, there was no way the FBI, the Army, or the Catholic Church could deny that something unusual had taken place in Maravilla. This something was stranger than Holy Air, as shattering as the Second Coming. It was well-documented; the whole world knew about it. This was not a hoax.

Father Ignatius was especially perplexed. He wasn't sure whether he should pray for the souls of the Giant Scorpions, or to deny that God had anything to do with it. The little priest saw the corpses of the Giant Scorpions, yet he refused to believe what he saw. He insisted it was a circus trick or an optical illusion. *What about the Person in White?* they asked the good friar. "Wha' person in whi'? I no see nobody in whi'." He flat out denied any such thing, although enough people saw it happen— locals and tourists both—that it was really not a question of whether but of *What the hell was that?*

Jake was shocked and bewildered. Tai-Keiko had landed in Maravilla for no particular reason. As he wrote it, he thought he would change it to a fictitious place; Maravilla was just a placeholder. But then the impossible happened: his story manifested itself in reality. While he was sitting at home writing the sequence about Tai-Keiko's battle with the Scorpions, the scene was actually playing out in real time and place. How was this possible? Was Jake channeling an alien power? Had Jake's computer been hijacked by cosmic hackers? He had heard the explosions and sirens and seen the smoke, but he had not yet connected the dots leading to his comic book yarn, where there were also explosions, sirens and smoke. *Just a weird coincidence,* thought Jake.

Nevertheless, he had to investigate. He wondered if someone had been hurt or needed help, so he jumped in his car and drove toward the plumes of smoke. He arrived at the scene ahead of the state police and was able to get a close look at the Scorpions. They were exactly as he had described them in his story. Jake stood there alongside Pilar and Archie and the others, gaping at the Creatures he had been writing about moments before. No one knew what to say, least of all Jake.

Little Luisa and her mother were awake, sitting on the ground and clutching each other in shock. Soon the volunteer fire department arrived and began to quell the flames of the burning police cars. Eventually more state troopers arrived and moved everyone back away from the dead Creatures.

Jake drove home in a daze. Upon reflection, though, he realized that he had seen Tai-Keiko taking off in her spacebug: a small smart zoomabout that had circled briefly overhead before whizzing away—just as he had written it. Could he actually control Tai-Keiko's destiny through his writing? There was only one way to find out, so when he got home he sat down to write.

Chapter IX, in which Tai-Keiko disguises herself and hides the spacebug

Tai-Keiko was in a dilemma. She could either search the wormhole for the proper portal that would take her to her own time and place on Earth, or she could stay where she was: on Earth before the Great Cataclysm. She had studied pre-Cat history in school, but being there and seeing it first-hand cast it in a different light. It was a paradise. Why human beings had degraded such a marvelous planet was a mystery. Ignorance, greed, maybe human nature? It had taken eons to rebalance it. Some habitats and species were lost forever.

Tai-Keiko realized that it would be a mistake to fly back to Maravilla and make a public landing in her spacebug. She would become a freak, a curiosity, a celebrity and never be able to live a normal life again. So she decided to hide the spacebug, find some casual clothing and go forth among the people. She landed on a hillside in a hidden spot, surrounded by juniper trees. Down below she could see a small house. She would pose as a tourist who had lost her way. She descended the hill, approached the house and knocked on the door.

To Be Continued . . .

Chapter Twenty-Two

Jake heard the knock and opened the door cautiously.

"I don't believe this," said Jake, who was barefoot.

"Sorry to bother you. I seem to have gotten lost," Tai-Keiko began.

"Tai-Keiko?" asked Jake. "Is your name Tai-Keiko?"

"Yes, but how. . ."

"My name's Jake. Jake Epstein. Please come in."

They shook hands. Tai-Keiko's hand felt real to Jake. Except for her white jumpsuit, she seemed totally normal. The jumpsuit was just as he had imagined it: a shiny silver-white that covered her body like a skin padded at the joints. Numerous buttons, slides and dials adorned the legs and chest.

"How's your wrist?" Jake asked, testing the waters.

"It's fine," replied Tai-Keiko haltingly. "Just a little sore."

"I suppose that's to be expected, having that quantum-chip in there for so long."

Tai-Keiko pulled her Laser-Luger from inside her jacket. "Another Krossarian? I just killed two of your Scorpions, and I can kill you too."

"Whoa! Hold on a minute," said Jake. "I'm not a Krossarian. I'm human; I *live* here."

Tai-Keiko looked around Jake's simple house. It was old and quaint. She shook her head in amazement. She pointed to Jake's computer on the table. "God only knows how old that thing is. Can't believe it still works."

"Tai-Keiko, do you know where you are?"

"I believe I'm in a place called Maravilla on planet Earth. But what year is it?" Jake told her. "Seriously? Then my suspicions were correct. I must have hit a crease in the space-time continuum and jumped back in time. The Krossarians just followed me through."

"Yeah, except that I made all that up. I created you," said Jake. "I know this is hard to believe; I'm having trouble with it myself. But I'm a writer. I wrote you into existence, and somehow you became real. Here. Read this." He handed Tai-Keiko the page he had just written.

Tai-Keiko read the page several times, trying to comprehend what was happening.

"How is it going to end?" she asked.

"I don't know. How *should* it end?"

"Well, I'd like to get back home—in the right year and the right place."

"Could you be more specific?"

"Oh, 2250, give or take a few years. When I travel at light speed, it messes with my inner calendar."

"And the place?"

"Elkhart, Indiana."

"I'll see what I can do."

***

After a week of intensive data-gathering by a gaggle of investigators, the quarantine was lifted and people were allowed back to their homes and shops. Teams of scientists spent many months and untold dollars analyzing the data, but eventually the FBI closed its investigation. Its conclusions were classified as Top Secret, which probably meant they couldn't substantiate any of their theories. But in Maravilla, theories were the lifeblood of the story, and they were told, debated, embellished, and marveled at for years to come.

Chapter Twenty-Three

Aurelio V was nothing if not nimble in business. When he saw an opportunity he took it, and if he was wrong he wasn't too proud to call off the project. Aurelio V was wrestling with the dilemma of whether to proceed with Gloryland or not. It was an expensive investment and a risky one. He knew that the locals were split on their view of Gloryland. He considered other uses for the property, such as a mobile home park or a retirement center.

But when the Creatures and the UFO visited Maravilla, Aurelio V saw his opportunity: Instead of Gloryland, a UFO museum. It would certainly be cheaper and carry less liability. The FBI had taken the dead aliens to the labs in Los Alamos for study, and had not released any details about them. But using digital animation, Aurelio V could recreate the Creatures and produce a short film of the showdown. He could play up the mysterious Figure in White: Where did it come from? Was it a hero or a villain? Alien or human? Where did it go? Why was it in Maravilla? If only Aurelio could get the backing of the locals, he would be unstoppable.

Aurelio V talked to his son about his new idea, and Aurelio VI was overjoyed. He was certain that Paloma and the local folks would be all smiles: the UFO Museum would still bring in tourists without offending the church patrons. It would also solve the problem of water use by eliminating the proposed water features.

The local kids thought it was cool. They didn't have a movie theater or even a playground, but they would have a UFO Museum. Some believers wondered whether God had created the aliens, but Father Ignatius saw no contradiction. The way he explained it, Maravilla had been blessed with a visit from the heavens. God was showing us that He could create multitudes of beings, all of whom can be redeemed through Jesus Christ, Our Savior. As for the Scorps, in rapid Spanish he explained how even dinosaurs and other extinct beings were creations of God, Lord of Heaven and Earth, although they had no souls.

"But Father," insisted one child, "if God can make ginormous bugs that can kill people, He must have made even ginormous-er birds to eat them."

"Yes, God tings of everything," agreed Father Ignatius. "Satan is the bug *y* God is the bird."

"Well, then, where are they?" persisted the child.

"Up there," said Father Ignatius looking skyward. "They lookin' for the bigges' bugges in the sky." The kids looked up in wonder.

Time proved Aurelio V right: tourists did come to see the UFO museum. In fact, the church and the museum provided an irresistible mix of the sacred and the mysterious, an enticing combination of the holy and the spooky, each one making the other more holy or spooky than it was by itself. People parked in the museum's large lot where they could buy a two-for-one ticket for the church and the museum. The price included a vial of Holy Air, blessed by the priest. The path, covered with palm fronds, connecting the church and the museum, was one of the few items that carried over from the plans for an amusement park. That, and the restrooms.

Across from the church was the living museum and gift shop, which pulled people in like a magnet pulls iron. Pilar was afraid that the Gloryland gift shop would decimate her business, but to her surprise, her business increased. She liked to say that Maravilla became a tourist destination, not a tourist trap. Because of the Salazars' parking lot and restroom facilities, the church was able to shut down their own misconceived restroom and remove the parking lot from the flood plain, leaving it as a place for birds and cattails.

Chapter Twenty-Four

Jake had created Tai-Keiko to be a character in a story, one among several characters, and he thought no more or less of Tai-Keiko than any of his other characters. At best, Tai-Keiko was a cartoon, drawn by a Japanese artist complementing Jake's evocative thought bubbles. She was not a superhero, but a figure of action and courage. Yet when Jake met Tai-Keiko in person, when he saw his creation manifested into flesh and blood, his feelings changed. Suddenly there was another person in the room besides Jake, a person with personality, power and a wily determination. And, no small detail, this other person was a woman. Jake had written Tai-Keiko as a woman at the request of the Japanese publisher, who believed that, in Japan, a woman action figure and superhero would sell better than a male would. The publisher had also specified that the hero be a young and beautiful Asian woman.

The Japanese cartoonist had given her rich and luxurious black hair, a strong and athletic figure, and intense, intelligent eyes. Helpless before such a woman, Jake fell in love with Tai-Keiko.

Jake had been in love twice before—with a woman first, and then a man—and he recognized the sweet obsession that clouds all judgment. In both of those cases, his love was unrequited. Despite his ardent courting, neither person fell in love with him. Jake was not a virgin, however. He had had casual flings when he lived in New York, but none of those affairs blossomed into a loving relationship.

Jake was surprised at his feelings for Tai-Keiko. Seeing her come off the page into the world was like meeting an entirely new person. Jake was bewildered by the metamorphosis, and it put him in the awkward position of having to choose between transporting Tai-Keiko to the year 2250, as she had requested and where she would be lost to Jake forever, or leaving her in the present where Jake could develop a relationship with her. This meant, Jake realized, that he would have a hand in shaping his own destiny; he would become responsible not only for Tai-Keiko's fate but for his own.

At the same time, Tai-Keiko was going through an intense discovery process as she realized she could talk and move by her own willpower and could feel emotions. To say the least, it was disconcerting to change so abruptly from an imaginary character, whose every move and word were scripted, to a real person with a body and mind of her own. She was unsure how much freedom she had, or if she really had any freedom at all. Her words and actions felt like her own, but at the same time Jake's writing suggested that she was a product of Jake's imagination.

At first, Tai-Keiko did not feel enamored of Jake. Tai-Keiko was grateful to Jake for creating her, but the idea of *amor* was not something she had ever considered. Sex and love had not been significant to her character—at least not yet. Tai-Keiko had no sexual feelings toward anyone, and she did not really distinguish emotionally between men and women. They were more like two colors in a painting: red and blue, purple and orange. He also realized that ultimately she had no control over her fate: Jake alone could determine that.

That first day, Jake had offered Tai-Keiko the couch for the night, and Tai-Keiko gladly accepted the offer. What were her other options? Find an empty barn or an abandoned house to hide out in until she could decide what to do? Neither option was very appealing.

So Tai-Keiko stayed the night at Jake's house, and in the morning Jake made waffles and served them with raspberries and maple syrup. Tai-Keiko had never imagined that something could taste so wonderful. Jake asked Tai-Keiko about her adventures en route to Zeton-9, and found, to his satisfaction, that they were just as he had written them. He read parts of the book to Tai-Keiko, who was astonished at the detail and accuracy of the action. It was then that Jake felt his heart open to Tai-Keiko, and this person he hadn't cared about, except as a device in his story, suddenly dominated his thoughts. For her part, Tai-Keiko was in awe of Jake and loved him the way a student loves a teacher or a mortal loves a god.

Jake asked Tai-Keiko if she would postpone her departure a few days, and Tai-Keiko said she would, although she felt she had no choice, since it appeared her future was entirely dependent on Jake's writing. But Jake showed no inclination to write, despite a steady stream of prodding emails from his agent. Instead, he eagerly showed Tai-Keiko around the countryside. They hiked through groves of aspens to a hot springs in the Jemez Mountains, and they marveled at the red cliffs of Ghost Ranch. They drove up to Taos through the Rio Grande Gorge. They rented horses and explored the Valles Caldera where they startled a herd of elk.

When they were at home, Jake taught Tai-Keiko how to cook and introduced her to the local *norteño* style of music. They spent virtually all their time together, blissfully for Jake, wondrously for Tai-Keiko. Tai-Keiko continued to sleep on the couch and Jake alone in his bed, until the first truly cold night, when the temperature dropped below freezing and they hadn't chopped enough wood for the stove.

"It's going to be cold tonight," said Jake. "Your blanket probably isn't warm enough. Why don't you sleep with me?" With the innocence of a child, Tai-Keiko got into Jake's bed and the pair of them cuddled up together, warm and content. Nothing happened of a sexual nature that night, and the next day, while Tai-Keiko was napping, Jake turned on his computer and wrote a new paragraph.

That night Jake invited Tai-Keiko to share his bed. He put on a recording of a velvet-voiced tanager from Brazil, an irresistible samba singer. Almost instantly she drew Tai-Keiko in

171

with her warm and comfortable tone, her speed and agility—all pitch-perfect. Jake slid in next to Tai-Keiko, and he put one arm around Tai-Keiko's shoulder and kissed her gently on the neck.

Jake stopped writing. "I can't do this," he muttered to himself. "I feel like I'm writing a romance novel. I don't write romance. I don't know *how* to write romance." He deleted the paragraph he had just written.

Jake wondered if he could jump straight to the ending. "And they lived happily ever after. The End." But no, he decided. Life is continuous; it doesn't jump over years; it travels through them. Time must be accounted for. And what about his blatant and crass attempt to have sex with Tai-Keiko by putting it into words first? "It's crap, that's what," Jake declared.

Ultimately, though, Tai-Keiko and Jake did have sex together. They did it the old fashioned way: with nervous, exploratory touches, tentative kisses, and mutual excitement. They didn't use Jake's magical writing, not even a word or a phrase. Jake's descriptions could never fully capture their rapture.

For Jake and Tai-Keiko, sex became a wonderful and ever-present backdrop—like richly ornamented drapes pulled across the front window. The days slid into weeks, and weeks into months. Tai-Keiko came to enjoy Maravilla, and was not a reluctant guest. "What was the hurry?" she asked herself.

Tai-Keiko and Jake became constant companions, seen everywhere together. They dropped into the bar scene in Santa Fe or Taos every now and then, but mostly stayed in Maravilla, finding fulfillment through each other. Tai-Keiko was a frequent source of gossip at Julio's *barberia*, especially being the only Asian woman in town. People wondered who she was and where she came from. The two of them became known around town as "Jake and that hippie chick." It didn't make sense, but it seemed to satisfy everyone.

Jake's writing lapsed. He didn't want anything to change. He was happy to leave the plot alone. His agent was furious, but Jake felt like this was a turning point in his life, and he couldn't mess it up by writing anything, unless he was absolutely sure it was the right course.

He realized that, in terms of his novel, and fiction in general, he couldn't let his love for Tai-Keiko change the focus of the book. To change the time and place in the middle of the story would be to hijack the plot. So Jake kept thinking about it, searching for a solution.

Tai-Keiko and Jake spent Christmas together—a complicated time for Tai-Keiko, who had to have everything explained to her. The ancient customs had long since disappeared from Tai-Keiko's world. They had died out everywhere but for some backwoods communities, though in their place was a new set of customs that were just as fantastic as the first. Nevertheless, Tai-Keiko enjoyed the wreaths and *ristras* and *farolitos*.

Now Tai-Keiko had been staying with Jake for several weeks, and Jake had still not written a word since he brought Tai-Keiko to his door. He began to wonder if he was keeping Tai-Keiko in Maravilla against her will. When asked, Tai-Keiko said that she was getting a bit homesick, but that she liked Maravilla very much.

"But it isn't only Maravilla that compels me to stay," Tai-Keiko said. "It's you. I feel such a strong attraction to you. I think you know that already, but I haven't said it out loud."

Jake had said it out loud dozens of times, but until now Tai-Keiko had always smiled and said something non-committal, such as "You're sweet," or "You make me feel so special." Once she said, "Oh Jake, it'll never work out for us. You're 250 years older than I am!" They giggled about that and made jokes for days about the difference in their ages.

Finally it occurred to Jake—and he couldn't figure out why he hadn't thought of it sooner—that perhaps Tai-Keiko didn't have to stay in Maravilla with him. Why couldn't the two of them fly off into an unknown future together? Why couldn't Tai-Keiko and he just disappear? It wouldn't be much different from a character being killed off in a murder mystery. However, there were some potential problems. Jake didn't know whether Tai-Keiko's little space ship was large enough or strong enough to spirit them away together. Or what if they ended up in different time periods, hundreds of years apart? One would die before the other was born.

That afternoon, while Tai-Keiko was napping, Jake introduced a new character in the story—namely, himself, a friendly, disheveled young man upon whose door Tai-Keiko knocked after the incident with the giant scorpions. Jake wrote quickly, devising an ending as he went.

An hour later, when he was done, he wrote an email to his agent: "Jennifer—Here is the end of the book. I hope it is sufficient. I'll be out of touch for awhile. Maybe forever. Thanks for everything. Jake."

Then he made a PDF of the new pages he had written, attached it, and hit "Send."

Chapter X, in which Tai-Keiko meets Jake

Jake was the perfect host, welcoming Tai-Keiko, inviting her in and offering her a meal. Tai-Keiko humbly accepted this hospitality, wondering if all Earthlings of this time period were as gracious. Before long, however, Tai-Keiko noticed an odd thing about Jake: He seemed to know a lot about her. He knew about the quantum-chip and her mission to Zeton-9. He knew about the Krossarians and their attempt to intercept Tai-Keiko and wrest the Formula from her. He even knew a little about the outer galaxies, which had not yet been explored in Jake's time. All this made her wary of Jake: perhaps he was a shape-shifting being from another time; perhaps he was an undercover Krossarian. Finally, she put the question out in the open.

"Jake," she said, fingering her Lasar-Lugar, "you seem to know all about me, although we've never met before. How can this be?"

Jake had expected this question. He had two answers: the truth, which was that he had no idea, or a lie, a barely believable explanation that he was a fortune teller, an oracle or a prophet who could foresee the future. He took a deep breath and told Tai-Keiko the truth.

"I don't know."

He told Tai-Keiko that he was writing an adventure story. The story was set in the future, but it followed an old formula: a hero sets off to accomplish a task and encounters many obstacles along the way.

"But how did you know the details of my journey?" Tai-Keiko asked.

"I don't know," Jake said again. "I thought I was making it all up."

Tai-Keiko was thoughtfully silent for a long time. Then she said, "Jake, I want to go home."

Jake didn't want her to go. "Why would you want to leave such a paradise as this?" he asked.

"Family, friends, favorite foods."

Jake asked, "Do you think I'd like it there?"

"I don't know. It's a controlled environment, of course. That's the way Earth is now, ever since the Great Cataclysm. It doesn't have the natural beauty of Maravilla."

Still, thought Jake, what an adventure! He had thought about this dilemma for days. He had thoroughly considered his next question and had decided to ask Tai-Keiko.

"Can I come with you?"

"You'd do that? Wow. It's risky, but it might be possible. I don't know what would happen to you going forward in time. Generally, we can only go backwards in time. I was born in 2225, and I'm 30, so I've already been in 2250. I wouldn't be going forwards in time. But you? For all I know, the magnetic plasma field could suck you right out of the spacebug and throw you into a canonical time loop."

"God forbid."

"Or it could result in chrono-spatial incoherence."

"What's that?"

"Well, at worst, your molecules would be scattered at random throughout the space-time continuum, and reconfiguring them to your current state would be next to impossible."

"Sounds dreadful. What are my chances of getting through safely?"

"Pretty good, actually. CSI is a rare phenomenon. More likely, your molecules will just vibrate momentarily before they return to normal."

"I suppose there's only one way to find out," Jake said, getting up. "Shall we risk it?"

Leaving everything in the house in quasi-chaos, dirty dishes on the table and soiled socks on the floor, Jake followed Tai-Keiko to where she'd hidden her spacecraft. It was a two-seater, with the pilot in front and a passenger seat behind. After chasing out a family of squirrels that had moved in, they climbed in and secured their ecto-plasmatic harnesses.

A moment later the small craft quietly lifted off. Anyone watching would have seen a white pod-like vehicle disappearing quickly into an enormous blue sky.

Chapter Twenty-Five

The state basketball tournament was played in Albuquerque at the UNM basketball arena, known as "The Pit." Tickets for Tuesday's playoff game went on sale a week before the game, and by noon of the second day all 17,000 seats were sold. Some of the thirty-dollar tickets had been bought by scalpers and were going online for one hundred dollars each. By Thursday those tickets were gone too.

On that fateful Tuesday many shops closed for the day, and there was an unusual spike in the number of government workers who called in sick from Rio Grande and Carson Counties. For residents of those counties, seeing their boys face each other in the Pit was better than seeing the championship game—better, in fact, than seeing any game from the Super Bowl to game seven of the World Series. The game had been scheduled for 2:00 p.m., and by eight in the morning, I-25 South was clogged with traffic. It looked like a sixty-mile funeral procession, cars creeping along bumper-to-bumper at thirty miles per hour. Rio Grande and Carson Counties emptied out like a horse corral with the gate left open.

Some people remembered to vote on Proposition 1 before they left for Albuquerque, but most did not. Perhaps they thought they would get home in time to vote—the polls were open from 7 a.m. to 7 p.m.—but even those who did get home in time to vote didn't feel like voting. They were either too depressed or too jubilant to care about the fate of Maravilla.

The residents of Maravilla, on the other hand, turned out in record numbers. The "Yes On 1" committee had organized a sophisticated get-out-the-vote campaign. Committee members had a list of every eligible voter in Maravilla and they knew which ones were "Yes" votes and which were "No" votes. They made sure that the "Yes On 1" block went to vote, whether they were going to the game or not.

There was no "No On 1" campaign to speak of. The commissioners waged this battle in the press, bombarding the media with dire predictions of what would become of Maravilla without the two counties. The residents would have no water rights, they would have no garbage pick up, no sheriff's department, no infrastructure. Maravilla would become a haven for criminals, a drug den, a sore on the body politic. Maravilla was not prepared to form its own county any more than the two counties were prepared to form their own state. If by some quirk or fraud there were more Yes votes than No votes, the two counties would go straight to the attorney general, not to some sagebrush judge who didn't understand the gravity of the situation.

The playoff game was a nail-biter all the way, with the lead changing hands every few minutes. The fans held their breath with every shot and cheered until they were hoarse. Both teams played their hearts out, and it wasn't until the end of the second overtime period that the Dust Devils pulled out a victory.

Meanwhile, the few remaining voters trickled into the voting booths to express their opinions. But it was not enough to defeat the insurgents. In the end, Proposition 1 passed 3645 to 2211.

Almost immediately, the two counties carried out their threat to appeal the lawfulness of the election, especially on the question of whether pets could be counted among the population. Not surprisingly, since the appellate judge was from Rio Grande County and in the thick of local politics, the election was nullified on the puzzling grounds that beings must be capable of committing acts with criminal intent before they can be considered individuals. Pets cannot break the law, said the judge's opinion, therefore they are not individuals. The attorney for Maravilla, Pete Gonzales, appealed this decision to the state Supreme Court.

Chapter Twenty-Six

Easter came early that year, at the end of March, and it snowed the night before. The consecration of the reconstructed church was scheduled to take place after Easter mass. Everything was made clean by the snow. By early afternoon the clouds had moved on and left behind a clear blue sky that sparkled off the snow and the whitewashed church. White apricot blooms glistened as the melting snow dripped from their branches.

Mass was at nine and eleven; the ceremony was set for one o'clock. Archie got there about nine-thirty to finish a few small welding jobs upstairs at the Visitor's Center. There was an Open House there after the ceremony.

Archie was not drunk that day, just careless. He had not turned the acetylene all the way off, and the pressure got high enough to cause spontaneous combustion, a small explosion that was hot enough to start a fire in the upstairs bathroom. At first the smoke floated out stealthily, not arousing any apprehension. By the time someone noticed, the smoke was pouring out the bathroom window and flames were flicking out under the eaves of the roof. The fire department got there as quickly as it could but was impeded by the amount of traffic that had come out from San Ramón and Truchas to see the consecration of the restored church. Cars were bumper to bumper, while pedestrians stood shoulder to shoulder. Some people tried to squirm their way toward the church, as others were pushing away from the burning house. The fire sirens did nothing but make the dogs howl and the babies cry. Eventually the fire trucks were engulfed in the gridlock too, and the diesel exhaust from their massive motors only added to the smoke drifting through the crowd, making people gasp for air, holy or otherwise. The firemen abandoned their trucks and dragged their heavy hoses through the crowds in the narrow streets. By the time water came coughing and spitting out the end of the hose, the top floor was already destroyed. What the fire didn't ruin, the water did.

Archie didn't know what had happened, but he was excited by the flames. He found a place to stand where he could watch it all unfold. Although he was fascinated by the fire, he found himself feeling sad that his metalwork would be ruined. He crossed himself and made a silent vow to be more careful in the future.

The main floor of the house was undamaged, so it could have been a lot worse. Still, for most people it put a pall over the day, scattering gray soot over the pristine snow and the white church, and making what should have been a joyous occasion into a grim reminder not to take anything for granted.

Chapter Twenty-Seven

It was Horacio who discovered that Jake had disappeared. He hadn't seen him around for a couple of weeks, which was unusual, so one day Horacio walked up to Jake's house and knocked. No answer. He walked around the house, looking in the windows, but saw nothing strange. Finally, he cracked the back door and called out, "Jake! Are you here, Jake?"

Getting no response, Horacio went in the house and began to search around, hoping for some sign that Jake had been there. But the dirty plates on the table were crusted with old food, the ashes in the fireplace were as dead as feathers, the sinks were dry and the bed was cold.

"This is odd," he thought. "That *pendejo* has his faults, but he wouldn't leave without saying goodbye." Horacio wondered if there was any foul play involved, but he wasn't ready to call the Sheriff yet. First, he asked around at Red's, at Pilar's shop, at Josie's Diner, at Julio's *barbería* . . . No one had seen Jake lately. Finally, he stopped in at the Post Office to ask Crystal if Jake had been in for his mail.

"Oh, sweet Jesus," said Crystal. "I completely forgot."

"Forgot what?" asked Horacio.

Crystal said, "Well, it's a strange thing, but about two weeks ago Jake came in with a pile of letters to mail. Wait a minute, I'll get them." Crystal disappeared in the back for a few moments and returned with a dozen identical-looking envelopes.

She said, "Jake came in and gave these to me, all stamped and ready to mail. But then he asked if I would hold onto them for a week before sending them out. I said why didn't he just come back in a week and mail them himself. He said he had to leave town and wasn't sure when he'd be back. He asked me, he said, 'If I don't come back for them in a week, would you please mail them for me?' I said that was highly unusual and probably against Post Office regs. He said, 'It probably is'—and everyone knows how I feel about following the rules—but could I make an exception, just this once? I said, 'Jacob, are you in trouble?' He said, 'No, it's nothing nefarious,' and I said, 'What's that mean, nefarious?' He said it meant 'evil.' 'I just want these envelopes to have a Maravilla cancellation stamp on them,' he said, 'and I probably won't be here to mail them myself.' I said, 'Why? You going on a trip?' 'You could say that,' he said, mysterious-like. And I said, 'Well, all right, but don't make a habit of it.' Then I stuck them on the top of a cabinet and completely forgot about them. Until now."

"Well, who are they addressed to?" asked Horacio.

Crystal said, "I can't tell you that. It's against the rules."

"Just give 'em here," said Horacio, and he grabbed the stack of letters out of Crystal's hands. Horacio looked through them quickly.

"Well?" Crystal demanded.

"Here's one for you," said Horacio, handing it to Crystal. "There's one for me, Pilar, Red, Paloma . . . . There's one for just about everyone. Maybe I should go deliver them."

"You don't have to do that," said Crystal. "What do you think the Post Office is for? Give those back to me."

Horacio handed over the stack of letters, and Crystal hand-cancelled them all. "Here," she said to Horacio. "This is yours. I'll distribute the rest of them."

Horacio took out his pocket knife and sliced open the letter.

"Dear Horacio," it said. "By the time you read this I'll be gone. I might be back, but I doubt it. Thank you for being such a great neighbor. I know you like my coffee pot, and I want you to have it to remember me by. But it only makes good coffee if you use good beans. Throw away that crappy canned stuff you use and buy some freshly ground beans. Take care of yourself. Best wishes, Jake."

Crystal put the rest of Jake's letters in with those to be delivered the next day. By the time they arrived, word had gotten out that Jake had gone away somewhere and that he had sent letters to some people in Maravilla, giving away his possessions.

He gave his car to Paloma, writing, "This is an early graduation present. Finish school and do something wonderful with your life. Believe it or not, this car gets good gas mileage, so you can drive up from Albuquerque every few weeks to see your mom and everyone else. I'm sorry the radio doesn't work. Also, it needs new wiper blades in case it ever rains again."

To Archie he wrote, "There's two old cars behind my house. They don't run, but they might provide some awesome parts for your sculptures. I'll ask Pete to help move them over to your trailer." Jake gave something to everyone he knew. His laptop and printer went to Pilar and Oscar ("In case you ever want to digitize your business"). Jake gave Red his eclectic set of cups and glasses, commenting "You really shouldn't be using plastic cups in such a classy place as yours." His ivory-handled letter opener he gave to Crystal. His acoustic guitar went to Sylvia with a note that said, "To accompany your beautiful voice." He gave away his radio, his kitchen knives and his cell phone. He asked Pete Gonzales to be the executor, the man in charge of distributing these possessions. "Anything that's left over, give it away to whoever needs it," he wrote to Pete. "And if I get any royalty checks from my book sales, use them to start a Maravilla Library fund."

The biggest gift was his house, which he gave to Alice. The thought of getting out of that cramped, mold-ridden, hot-in-the-summer-cold-in-the-winter metal box—and into a real adobe house with a view—moved Alice to tears.

To Aurelio VI Jake gave nothing but some advice. "If you really love Paloma, encourage her to graduate and then let her follow her dream. It may lead to you. I'm no expert in affairs of the heart, but sending her flowers once in a while might help too."

***

Later that year the New Mexico Supreme Court ruled that "individuals" meant individual people, and that pets, being owned by people and never responsible for themselves, could not be considered "individuals" under the law. However, the Court also ruled that Maravilla was an entity with its own identity, distinct from either Rio Grande or Carson Counties, and that it therefore would be granted a special status as an historical district within the two counties, entitled to its own post office.

There was much rejoicing over this decision, for most of the people of Maravilla did not want to take on the burden of self-governance anyway. They only wanted Maravilla to be recognized as the special place it was and still is to this day.

Coming Soon!

DANGEROUS CROSSING
by
R. Douglas Clark

It looked like a simple case of blackmail for sexual misconduct. But when Eddie Maez, a prize-winning journalist, is asked to investigate, he finds himself dragged into a thicket of drug smuggling, human trafficking and illegal sports betting in the treacherous borderland of south Texas. Caught in a web of greed, secrets, lies and deceit, Eddie must find a way out. But in this underworld where human life has little value, who can he trust?

**For more information
visit:** www.SpeakingVolumes.us

On Sale Now!

A suspenseful must read, *Defense Mechanism*.

For more information
visit: www.SpeakingVolumes.us

On Sale Now!

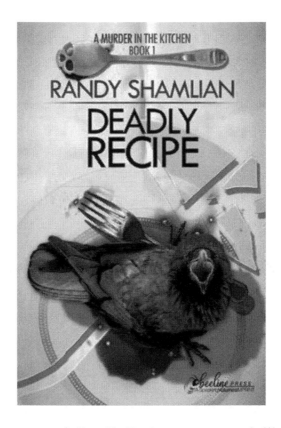

A must-read, ***Deadly Recipe***, a suspense thriller.

**For more information
visit:** www.SpeakingVolumes.us

Sign up for free and bargain books

Join the Speaking Volumes mailing list

Text

ILOVEBOOKS
to 22828 to get started.

Message and data rates may apply.

56069533R00116

Made in the USA
Middletown, DE
22 July 2019